$\mathcal{I}$ hopped out of the bubble, nearly stepping into the bathroom wall. "Oof," I said, turning around to see a mirror. I swallowed another squeal. There I was, starring as Floressa Chase in a green striped bikini, dark shades resting on my head. I flipped her black hair and smiled over my shoulder. There were thousands of girls who would love to be Floressa Chase. I was the only one, besides her, who actually was.

Also by Lindsey Leavitt

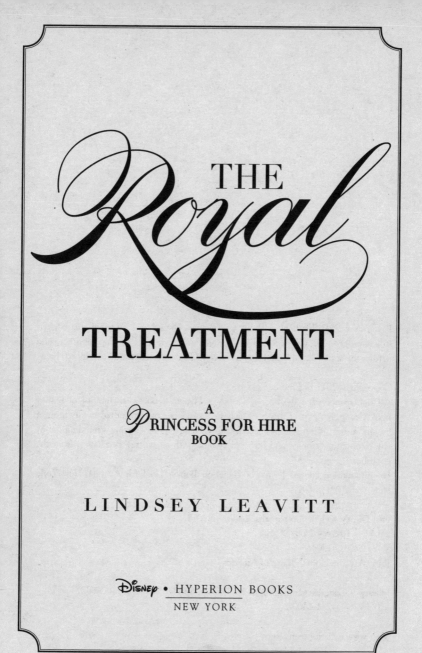

THE
Royal
TREATMENT

A
PRINCESS FOR HIRE
BOOK

LINDSEY LEAVITT

DISNEP • HYPERION BOOKS
NEW YORK

Copyright © 2011 by Lindsey Leavitt
All rights reserved. Published by Disney • Hyperion Books, an imprint of Disney Book Group. No part of this book may be reproduced or transmitted in any form or by any means, electronic or mechanical, including photocopying, recording, or by any information storage and retrieval system, without written permission from the publisher.
For information address Disney • Hyperion Books, 114 Fifth Avenue, New York, New York 10011-5690.

First Disney • Hyperion paperback edition, 2012
1 3 5 7 9 10 8 6 4 2
V475-2873-0-12046
Printed in the United States of America

Library of Congress Cataloging-in-Publication for Hardcover: 2011004802
ISBN 978-1-4231-2300-2

Visit www.hyperionteens.com

To Mom and Dad

Chapter

I

"Hot Cross Buns" has to be one of the stupidest songs in the history of music. You want some buns. They're a penny. Please buy them and shut up about it, so we don't have to go over the same three notes. I shuddered to think how the next song, "Twinkle, Twinkle, Little Star," was going to sound. Small children would cry.

"Okay." My best friend, Kylee Malik, tried to paste on an encouraging smile, but the corners of her mouth didn't fully commit. "You know that song Michael Jackson used to sing? 'ABC'? If you can sing that in your head, you'll remember the notes for 'Hot Cross Buns.'"

"Wait, why would I use *another* song to remember this

song?" I gripped the neck of my rented violin. "The notes I remember; I just don't know how to *play* them."

"Can I be an honest friend, then?" She scooted my music stand to the side. As the band director's special assistant, Kylee was supposed to be using the high school music room for her own rehearsals, but she'd snuck me in as favor.

"Yes. Shoot."

"Maybe you should, you know, quit." Her eyes widened. "Not that you don't have, er, talent! Just not with this. What if we rehearsed for the play tryouts on Monday instead?"

"I still don't know if I want to audition. It's Shakespeare. And a *high school* play. My chances are one in twenty thousand."

"I may not be a math whiz, but I'm pretty sure they're better than that. This isn't some fine-arts school in New York. It's Sproutville. Idaho. There'll be fifty, sixty, people trying out. Tops. And it's technically a junior high *and* high school play, so you have as much of a chance as a senior."

"Whatever." The school district was only letting the junior high students try out because they cut our theater program. Sorry, "merged" us with the high school. Seniors were still going to have, well, *seniority* over eighth graders.

"And you're good, Desi. Honest."

I played with the hem of my self-designed NOTEWORTHY T-shirt, hoping Kylee couldn't tell how much I wished that she was right. I'd wanted to be an actress since I'd seen my first Audrey Hepburn movie when I was nine. I couldn't count how many nights I'd stayed up, reciting classic movie lines to my bedroom mirror. Probably close to the number of times I'd read through the fall play, Shakespeare's *A Midsummer Night's Dream*. But that familiar longing wasn't as important as my immediate musical need. "I can work on lines tonight. Right now, I want to become Beethoven."

"Um . . . so *that's* probably never going to happen, especially with the violin. Maybe we haven't found your instrument yet. There's the . . . the xylophone."

"My sister, Gracie, plays the xylophone. She's two. Am I that bad?"

Kylee frowned. "No, I mean, well . . . *bad* is such a *strong* word."

"Kylee, you're being the honest friend, remember?"

"It sounded like a barrel of cats playing tubas. In B-flat."

"What is B-flat?"

Kylee covered her mouth, but she couldn't escape the snort that came out.

"You're laughing?" I pointed my bow at her. "My musical dreams have come to an end and you're *laughing*?"

"Musical dreams?" Kylee kept giggling. "You just decided you wanted to learn an instrument last month."

"Maybe it was a *secret* dream."

"If you care that much, we'll keep working on it. But you're going to lose an eye waving that bow around."

"Fine. We'll give Mr. Violin a break. But I'm blaming all failure on you, teach."

I tucked the violin into its case—my favorite part of practicing. So the musical dream was bogus, but I did have *princess* dreams, and if I wanted to return to my magical job with the royal substitution agency, Façade, I had some training to do.

Last summer, an agent named Meredith Pouffinski popped—and I mean *popped* (she travels by bubble)—into my bathroom and told me that Façade detected my MP—magic potential—when I made a wish on some magical fish. The MP could transform me into the exact look-alike of any princess in need of a vacation. All I had to do was sign a contract and apply the ancient Egyptian formula Royal Rouge. *Poof!* Princessified.

Of course I took the job—who wouldn't want to travel the world, meet royals, and make loads of money doing it? But I found that princesses often "vacationed" during crazy times, leaving me to deal with everything from Amazon tribal festivals to heinous diet plans. And although it complicated my job more, I really made an effort to positively impact the princesses's lives while impersonating them. My goal to impact went too far when I kissed Prince Karl because I knew my client, Elsa, was too shy to do it herself. This choice nearly lost me my amazing job, but in the end, the Court of Royal Appeals (the big honchos of Façade) endorsed my advancement to Level Two—a privilege I *needed* to prove I deserved.

A few days after returning from my subbing adventures, a package arrived for me in Idaho. I was elated to find my princess-sub manual inside—a handheld touch-screen computer thingy that had everything about royals I ever wanted to know. Except now that I'd moved up to Level Two, there was a message saying I had to go through something called Betterment of Elite Sub Training.

Betterment of Elite Sub Training (BEST . . . these people loved their acronyms) was simply a list of things I needed to *develop* before I could sub for my first—still unrevealed—Level Two princess. Each job included a new list, and my first one included . . .

1. Classical music, understanding and mastery. Instrumental abilities (woodwinds and strings) highly encouraged.
2. European courtly dances of the eighteenth and nineteenth century
3. History of French royalty, particularly the period before and immediately after the French Revolution
4. Eighteenth-century art history and architecture, with an emphasis on the baroque style
5. Public speaking, as well as conversational skills

So I'd spent the summer looking through art slides, reading *A Tale of Two Cities*, attempting to play the violin, watching online videos of people prancing around in period costumes, and delivering my favorite speeches from old movies to Gracie's stuffed-animal collection (okay, so the public speaking still needed work). It was mid-September now, a couple of weeks into school. I was doing fine, but I had no clue when I would be *done*. I wouldn't know it was time until Meredith dropped in with her bubble. I could return to my dream job any day.

I buckled the case shut and surveyed the music room. There really was a xylophone in there. Was the xylophone a classical instrument? Was the BEST musical point going to be the one task that kept me from returning to Façade?

"Hey, Kylee, what if I did play the xylophone? Or the flute! Flutes are fancy. And, um, woodwinds, right? And can I learn about B-flat and allegro and forte and all that music stuff?"

"Okay, I'll teach you the flute if you tell me why you're suddenly interested in music *stuff*." Kylee shook her finger. "And don't tell me it's a hidden dream. A few weeks ago, all you wanted to do was watch old movies, and now it's like you're training to be a debutante."

Debutante. Yikes . . . not too far away from princesses, actually. And welcome to Desi's Daily Balancing Act, which involves me conversing with my new best friend without telling her my biggest secret. Not only would she not believe me, but I'd signed a contract promising not to share any information about the Façade Agency.

"Fine. I'll reveal my deep dark secret." I grabbed a mallet and dinged a xylophone key, hoping I came off as breezy. "*After* you teach me the flute."

"We only have five minutes before my practice session ends. I think another group booked the room."

"Five minutes. Deal. And I'll buy us some Slurpees after."

Kylee found a school-owned flute in the music closest and held up the mouthpiece. "So the hard part is getting your mouth right. Purse your lips together like you're blowing on soup."

I made a blowing-on-soup face, not an easy task with braces.

"Good, now, before I attach the rest of the flute, you need to get your blow down." She shoved the cold metal mouthpiece under my lips.

"Whoa. Slow down with the blow down."

"Ha-ha. Here. Remember, soup blow."

I held the instrument up to my mouth, picturing a nice clam chowder. But when I blew, it sounded more like a windy raspberry.

Kylee cringed. "So, that would be your . . . starting point."

I blew out again, more in exasperation than in an attempt to create music. The raspberry sound only got wetter.

I glared at the mouthpiece. So, this instrument thing? Kind of a stupid idea. Seriously, what was I thinking? It takes people YEARS to learn an instrument. And I had to get back to work soon! Maybe if I listened to Mozart, 24-7, it would seep into my fingers. Yes, the osmosis approach. And the BEST list said "highly encouraged," not "completely necessary." Besides, I'd subbed for a musical princess during my

7

Level One days, and I made it out of that okay. So what if her instrument had been destroyed in the process?

Kylee was right. Instruments weren't my thing. I would brainstorm another plan tonight. Time for Slurpees.

I screwed on the other two parts of the flute and blew hard. "Okay, I'm done. But, wait. Look!" I pretended like I knew how to play notes, jiggling the pinky key with force. "I'm a natural! Call me the Pied Piper."

Kylee laughed, covering her ears while I started a little jig. I was getting into it, twirling around, my fingers flying across the keys. The violin was ear heaven compared to my flute sounds. I almost didn't hear someone whistling. Whistling? I looked at Kylee, but her face was frozen in horror.

Standing in the doorway was my former best friend, Celeste Juniper, and behind her stood about twenty other kids.

Tall, mature kids. High school theater kids.

Celeste's eyes glinted in triumph. "Sorry to interrupt . . . well, I think that was a solo. Or maybe an audition for *Cats*. You have the screeching sound *perfect*."

"We booked this room for our thespian meeting." A short guy in a cardigan started to move chairs. "Hope that's cool."

The flute was still perched in the air, like an antenna signaling my lameness. I told my elbow to lower, but elbow did not listen. Everyone else filed in, pushing chairs into a circle that was now forming around me. Kylee finally grabbed my arm and pulled me to a corner of the room. "No problem.

8

We were just working on a comedic scene for Desi's audition. She's auditioning for the play."

The rest of the thespians, thankfully, ignored us and began their vocal warm-ups. No such luck with Celeste. "So you're auditioning?" she asked. "How many plays have you tried out for?"

"Four," I answered softly.

"And how many have you been cast in?" Celeste asked.

"Zero," I said, my voice even softer. Wait. I wasn't going to let Celeste make me feel invisible. She'd been awful to me for the last two years because my lawyer dad sent her guilty dad to jail. TWO YEARS AGO. "Zero plays, but things are different now."

"Yeah. And the fifth time is the charm," Kylee added.

Old Desi would have vaporized right then. But old Desi washed away over the summer, and now I could be the person I always wanted to be. Besides, I'd already embarrassed myself with the Flute Boogie. Auditions couldn't be any worse. "I *am* trying out. I'll see you there. And good l uck."

"It's bad luck to say 'good luck' to an actress."

"I know. That's why I said it." I took Kylee's hand so we could make a dramatic exit, but she was firmly rooted to the spot. Celeste smirked and walked back to the warm-up circle.

"We were supposed to make an exit just then," I said.

"Look," Kylee said in a fierce whisper. "Over there. Reed Pearson."

Sure enough, Kylee's new crush was in the circle, repeating lines with a partner. His voice, or maybe it was his New Zealand accent, rang louder than the others. When he caught us staring, he waved.

"I can't go over there," Kylee said. "I haven't even practiced."

"Practiced what?"

"Practiced talking to him." She shot a desperate glance at the door. "I mean, he's so cute and older than us—"

"Only one year older—"

"I'm going to go. Call me tonight." Her nails cut into my skin. "And I want details."

Reed strode across the room as Kylee zipped out. "Did I scare her away?" he asked.

"No. Well, yes." I shook my head. "She has a deep fear of thespians."

He laughed. "We aren't contagious."

I was about to make a joke about thespianitis, but then I felt bad that I was the one laughing with him, and not Kylee. So I didn't say anything. The silence went stale, and Reed cleared his throat. "So, I'm Reed. We met over the summer when—"

You saved my life by administering CPR after I almost drowned in a dunk tank, which involved our mouths touching, which is why I am having a very difficult time forming sentences right now. "I remember." Another endless beat of empty air, then, "So are you trying out for the play?"

"No, I came for your concert earlier."

I felt my face flame. "Yeah . . . that. Interpretive dance."

"Well, whatever it was, I thought it was original."

"Thanks."

"You'll be at auditions, right?" he asked.

"Uh . . . I think so."

"Good."

Reed's friend called him over. I was about to say something more, something about Kylee, but he was already moving away. He held up his elbow, his fingers tapping an invisible instrument. "Bye, flute girl."

I got out of there, glancing around the hallway for Meredith, in case by some bizarre miracle my violin and/or flute playing had been enough to complete my BEST. My bravado with Celeste was already dying, and now that I'd committed to auditions, I wanted out of Sproutville fast.

Like, magical bubble–speed *fast*.

Chapter 2

"How many cartons of ice cream do you *need?*" Mom asked as I chucked flavor after flavor into our shopping cart. When I'd come home looking upset, she'd left Gracie with Dad and drove me to the grocery store for a "little stress treat." I guess she'd underestimated my level of stress.

"You have that extra freezer in the garage." Cookies and cream, pistachio . . . what was caramel explosion? Didn't matter. Into the cart.

"That's part of our food storage. For emergencies."

"It's been one of those days."

"Did your dad make a comment about your work ethic again?"

"No. He's been quiet about that since I told him

how much I was making with my T-shirt Web site." I pretended to read the label on the chocolate-fudge-ripple carton so Mom wouldn't see my face. My lying face. I'd only sold, um, five T-shirts. But I needed an excuse to quit my pet store job, so I'd showed Dad some of my subbing money to prove I was still saving for college, which is a gazillion years away. (Yeah, I know, he's no joke.) It's not that I hated Pets Charming, it's just that I had to focus on my BEST points, and school was starting and maybe the play and . . . okay. So I hated that job. Some of my clothes still smelled like cat throw-up.

"So what's going on?" Mom blocked me from loading any more ice cream. "Do you want to talk about it?"

"It's nothing." I shrugged. "I acted like an idiot in front of half the high school theater department. Oh, and your best friend, Celeste, was super nice to me about it. As always."

"Honey, were you nice to her? Sometimes you get on a sarcastic kick and she naturally gets a little defensive—"

"Mom, she *attacked* me."

I waited for my mom to smooth my hair and say, *Of course she did. She is a liar, just like her jailbird father, and you, Desi, are the daughter of my dreams! Buy as much ice cream as you want.* But she didn't, because my mom attends Camp Every Story Has Two Sides, which is great in a Disney Channel movie but not so helpful when I needed a listening ear.

"Desi—"

"Anyway," I said. "Whatever. I don't even care."

"I've been meaning to talk to you about Celeste." Mom finally did smooth my hair down, but her hand felt heavy on my head. "Are you really okay with me being her consultant for Miss Teen Dream?"

Was I okay with Celeste's two-month-long pageant training happening at *my* house with *my* mom while the girl ate *my* vanilla wafers? Gee, why wouldn't I be? I only had to witness their annoying girlie bonding for a few more weeks until the pageant started in October, but I was close to my limit. Last Tuesday, I'd come home to them giggling over a bowl of cookie dough.

"What? That?" I asked. "Of course. I mean, you know I think pageants are—"

"The demise of society. Yes. Which is why I didn't ask if you wanted to participate. Should I have asked you?"

"Seriously, I am so busy lately, a pageant would . . ." I tried hard not to laugh, because I knew my mom was being sincere. A *pageant*? Smearing Vaseline on my teeth and wearing a strapless bra and solving world peace? "It's not my thing. And I'm fine with your emcee and consultation jobs— you have the personality and you're great with fashion."

"But . . ."

"But I don't feel the same about Celeste." I pushed our cart over to the checkout. "I just don't. I don't, like, *hate* her or anything, but it still isn't easy seeing you two have your girlie fests every day."

"Girlie fests?"

"Makeovers. Dress shopping. Coaching Celeste's interview answers."

"But you said you don't like pageants."

"I don't! But I still like you." I unloaded my ice cream onto the checkout counter "Look, why are we even talking about this? I'm fine with us. And Celeste isn't a big deal— I'm just stressed about the play. I need to get home and read over the second act."

"I'm sorry." Mom touched my arm. "Why don't I help you practice tonight?"

"Really? It's Shakespeare. Pretty boring—"

"I love Shakespeare and I love you." She kissed my forehead. Yep. In public. "We'll even have our own girlie fest. Why don't you pick out a magazine to go with your ice cream? Oh! And I'll paint your nails. Get some hair dye . . . Have you ever thought about highlights? Your brown has some beautiful gold undertones we could play up."

"Let's start with ice cream and magazines," I said. "And that cookies and cream is all mine . . ." My voice trailed off when I noticed the magazines in the checkout aisle.

Well, one *particular* magazine. Staring back at me from a glossy tabloid was . . . was . . . him.

Prince Karl of Fenmar.

And he was laughing with Elsa.

"Holy royals." I yanked the magazine off the shelf and flipped to the article, nearly ripping out the pages in my frenzy. The picture was on page 39, after the newest interview with celebutante Floressa Chase.

Karl looked adorably stiff as he leaned against a speckled brown horse. Elsa had her arms folded across her chest, one toe pointed in the muddy grass. The sky was gray, the colors dull; but Karl and Elsa smiled at each other as if they lived on a rainbow. No one else was around them, so it seemed they'd stolen this moment alone and a paparazzo had captured it.

"Honey, you look like . . . like you saw a picture of yourself in there."

Laughing together. Together. The two of them were spotted at a polo match, laughing together like old friends.

I ran my finger down the lines of print.

> *Did longtime friends Prince Karl and Princess Elsa spark a romantic relationship in Metzahg earlier this summer? Princess Elsa could not be reached for comment, but Prince Karl's publicist stated that although the prince is indeed friends with Elsa, he is still happily dating Duchess Olivia. Karl and Olivia were spotted at Crown Prince Jasper's christening last week, and the couple continues to be of great interest in royal circles.*
>
> *Regardless of what her relationship with the prince may be, it seems Princess Elsa's famously eccentric grandmother, Princess Helga of the former Royal House of Holdenzastein, had a change of heart regarding Elsa's role in the royal community. Princess Elsa's fall calendar will include exclusive regal events, though her schedule has yet to be announced.*

I knew there was some truth to the rumor about Elsa and Karl, because I had been there, in Metzahg, as Elsa's sub. I'd solidified their romance by kissing Karl after reading about Elsa's devotion to him in her journal. This was the kiss that had almost cost me my job, but reading the article proved that my instincts had been right—they did like each other.

But as noble as my matchmaking seemed, I had a secret. A tiny piece of me wondered . . . maybe even hoped . . . that Karl's feelings had deepened during my time with him. That he liked me too, although, obviously, he had no clue I existed.

The whole thing made my brain, not to mention my heart, hurt. I handed the magazine to the checkout lady. Mom grabbed another copy from the rack and thumbed through it. "That's the prince that's all over your bedroom wall now, right? His brother is much cuter. And who is the girl?"

"Princess Elsa of the House of Holdenzastein," I said automatically.

"Wow. You're very . . . knowledgeable."

"I read it in the article. And besides, Prince Karl *is* cute, just not in an obvious way."

She turned the page to the side. "Well, maybe he has a nice personality. He's a little on the short side—"

"He's five feet seven. Perfectly average!" I almost shrieked, ripping the magazine from her hand.

"Okay, sure." Mom held up her hands. "I didn't know you'd become such a crazy fan."

While she paid for the ice cream and magazine, I glanced at the picture of Karl one more time. "I'm not crazy. I'm buying a magazine."

"If you say so."

"Seriously. Let's go home. If I don't get over my nerves, I'll be lucky to make Tree Number One."

Chapter 3

*H*aving abandoned any hope of learning an instrument in this century, I went with Plan B and spent the rest of the weekend listening to an extensive classical music playlist and scrolling through my manual to see if I could find anything more about Karl and Elsa's encounter. All I managed to find about Elsa were the notes I'd submitted last June to the sub chat room, a place where you can usually find dirt on royals that even the magazines don't know. The Karl stuff was a repeat of the usual tabloid chatter: his relationship with Duchess Olivia, his work with the AFRICA IS HUNGRY foundation, the scandals of his ridiculously good-looking and pompous older brother, Barrett. I knew that information already. The question I kept asking myself was: *What is going* on *between Karl and Elsa?* And the quieter, mixed-up question behind it: *What does it have to do with me?*

The royal drama also kept me from stressing about the audition. Okay, not true. I was *beyond* stressed. Now that I'd had so much practice "acting" as a princess, I secretly hoped I'd get a role. Nothing big—maybe a small speaking part. Before Façade, I'd never dared to believe my acting dream could be a reality. Anytime I'd tried out before, it was almost to prove to myself that I couldn't make it.

Now I knew anything was possible. Possible, but not guaranteed.

I tried to explain my audition angst to Kylee when she met me at my locker after school on Monday, but every time I opened my mouth, it sounded like a gurgle.

"You ready?" she asked.

I gurgled yes.

"Drink some of my water. You need to stop that weird moaning sound every time you talk."

I took a swig of her water and cleared my throat. "It's a gurgle."

"It's gross."

"I can't believe I'm doing this." I drank some more water. "I'm going to pass out on the stage."

"Maybe that'll get you a part. Pretend like you're falling asleep—that's perfect for *A Midsummer Night's Dream*." Kylee pushed me out the doors and into the front quad. Our steps fell into sync as we hit the sidewalk that separated the junior high from the high school. "Besides, you've done this before."

"I've tried out for a play before, but I've never gotten a part. And those plays were not Shakespeare."

Confession time: this probably makes me sound dumb, or just not deep, but I don't love Shakespeare. Sure, the stories are great, but why keep it in ancient words that everyone pretends to understand, but no one actually does? I'm guessing I'm not alone in my feelings, but if you admit this, it's like saying you don't see the emperor's new clothes. Loving Shakespeare makes you literary and artsy cool, two traits that are an edge in the performing-arts world. Funky hats help, too—all the theater kids had them. I didn't bring one, but I was wearing a SHAKESPEARE ROCKETH shirt. I figured that might earn me some street cred.

"Shakespeare is like anything else, with some *thees* and *thines* mixed in," Kylee said.

"Don't forget the *aye* and *ere*. Do you think people used to fall asleep in the middle of conversations?" I stopped walking when we rounded the corner. Sproutville High—ivy-draped red brick, built in the 1930s and an easy double for an insane asylum—loomed before us. "I can't do this. Let's go home."

"Nope. You're doing it." Kylee pulled me forward. "Here, tell me your monologue."

"We weren't supposed to prepare anything. The director tells us what we're reading at the audition."

"Just say something."

I delivered a line, one that I'd memorized from the second act.

"See?" Kylee beamed. "You're going to get a part, I know it. The words make *sense* when you say them."

"Whatever. Shakespeare is probably rolling in his grave every time I read."

"Who made up that expression anyway?" Kylee said. "Why is rolling in your grave bad? Maybe it means you're a zombie or something. If your acting creates a Shakespeare zombie, I'd be all for that. Like, he could come on the stage during all his plays and be like . . . 'Iambic pentameter . . . bad. Brains . . . good.'"

I scrunched up my nose. "You've been watching too many of those gross horror movies again."

"Better that than your old Audrey what's-her-name movies."

"What's-her-name? *What's-her-name?* Audrey Hepburn is only one of the greatest actresses to ever live on this planet. Or any planet. Oh my gosh, if I were in my grave right now, *I* would be rolling."

"Doesn't work if you're still breathing. Then you're buried alive, and that's just sad—"

"ROLLING!" I yelled. Kylee giggled.

I don't know when it happened, but somewhere between June and now, Kylee and I had reached that wonderful *place*. The one where you know things about each other that no one else does. Even more, you accept them.

Like, Kylee's so cultured, if she had MP she'd probably

skip over Level One and settle right into Level Two at Façade. She moved to Sproutville a year ago from Seattle with her professional, smart, cool parents (from *India*. My dad is from Idaho Falls. If there was a contest for coolness, her parents would get the grand-prize trophy and mine a nice participant ribbon). The Maliks take their daughter to exhibits and the symphony and poetry readings. But cute, clean-cut Kylee is also hard-core into horror movies and gory video games. Isn't that awesome? I love that about her.

We walked around the building, stopping at the theater entrance door. Kylee gave my arm a squeeze. "So I'm going to run over to the band room to make sure that the woodwinds workshop I'm teaching next week is all set up."

"Uh-huh."

"And then I'll be back in time to watch you try out."

"Right." I turned and stared at the doors.

"Desi!" she said. "Go in!"

The lobby air-conditioning hit me with a blast. I folded my arms over my chest, perspiration forming despite the new chill. The sign on the theater door, DISTRICT PLAY TRYOUTS, made me sweat even more. Man, I wished they'd kept the junior high theater program. Now, on top of attempting all those *thees* and *thines*, I had to try out with teens old enough to drive.

Teens old enough to vote.

Old enough to grow Shakespeare-worthy beards.

A few frozen seconds later, I noticed Reed sitting at the

table by the trophy case. His head was down, his pencil tapping to the music coming from his headphones. His black hair fell into his eyes, contrasting nicely with his tan skin. I dug a pen out of my backpack and signed the audition sheet in front of him. Had Kylee been there, the smile he flashed would have melted her into a pool of girliedom. Of course, I was immune to it. Pretty Boy in Idaho didn't compare to Kind, Sweet Prince in Europe.

"Glad you decided to come," Reed said. Sorry. Pretty Boy in Idaho with a hot accent. "Where's your flute?"

"Um, I'm trying to get a part, not make the director scream in terror."

"Then don't say *um*. It's Mrs. Olman's pet peeve."

"Um, thanks. I mean, oops, I already failed." I read over the audition sheet. Introduction, stage movement, and choose one of the three provided monologues. Five minutes of talking, if that. Some of my princess substitute jobs lasted for *days*. I could manage five minutes.

I looked up to see Reed watching me, so I searched my mind for something to say. "Are you an assistant? Why are you doing sign-ups?"

"Because I'm a lowly freshman."

"If you're lowly, then what are the eighth graders?"

He laughed. "I'm not going to answer that. I can tell you what some seniors think about the junior high jumping into our play."

"Jumping in? Yeah, right. It wasn't *our* choice. And you guys have the advantage."

"Oh, absolutely. There're only a few seventh and eighth graders who showed up. I bet most got freaked by the whole high-school-Shakespeare thing. The chances of you actually making it are slim to none. Probably closer to none."

I scuffed my left foot across the tile floor. "Thanks for the vote of confidence."

"Oh, I didn't mean . . ." Reed closed his eyes. "Sorry. Sometimes I don't think before I talk. Even if it's the truth."

"So the truth is I shouldn't even bother to audition."

"No! It's just, *statistically*, your chances might be lower. But if you're a good actress, that's not going to matter. And you don't seem very nervous." Reed fixed me with an intense stare. "Are you?"

I couldn't make eye contact when he looked at me like that, like he was trying to hypnotize me to tell the truth. Whew, no wonder Kylee fled from him in the band room.

"Nervous? Me?" A good actress would have faked confidence right then. But I was too busy counting all the names on the sign-up sheet, each signature another chance I wouldn't make it. Over fifty people auditioning for a play with maybe twenty parts. "No, I'm not nervous. I'm . . . I'm terrified." I slumped my shoulders. "I've been reminding myself to breathe all day."

"Hey, no worries." Reed's expression softened. "Everyone is nervous. Some people are just better at covering it up."

"Like you?"

"Oh yeah. I already threw up once."

"No way."

"Sure. But I brushed my teeth, so now I'm minty fresh." Reed glanced at the clock and stood. "I think that's probably it for sign-ups. I'm going in, if you want to come. It's always nice to have an audition buddy."

Buddy. Oh no. Kylee. Two conversations with the kid, and I still hadn't mentioned Kylee. "Yes! My friend Kylee is coming. She plays the clarinet. And, like, every instrument. And she's really fun and cute."

Reed slipped the sign-up sheet under his arm. "Sorry, so is *she* your audition buddy? I don't want to break a sacred circle here."

"No, I mean, save two seats—one for me, and one for Kylee. I'm going to go over this monologue for a minute."

"Cool." Reed leaned against the door and pushed it open with his back. "Oh, and make sure you say your name right when you're on the stage. Mrs. Olman said you might as well quit now if you can't do that."

"Thanks for the added pressure."

"Any time."

The door slammed shut, the sound echoing through the theater lobby. *Terrified*—that word wasn't big enough. If I psyched myself out any more, my heart was going to jump out of my chest and start quoting Shakespeare. I read through the monologues four or five times, deciding on the Helena part, then slipped into the theater.

It took a moment for my eyes to adjust and find Reed in the back right corner.

"Did I miss anything?" I asked.

"They already started," Reed whispered. "She's doing it alphabetically. What's your last name?"

"Desi Bascomb?" Mrs. Olman's voice rang out across the auditorium.

"Uh, here?" I waved.

"Yes, well, we'd like you *there*." She pointed to the stage.

So much for having some time to calm down. I hurried down the aisle, noticing Celeste sitting in the second row with my former crush, Hayden. Hayden stared at me blankly, which I didn't take personally since I was beginning to realize that *blank* was his specialty.

Celeste had undoubtedly wrangled Hayden into auditioning with her. If any eighth grader was going to get a part, it would be her—she'd always made the school and community plays in the past. No, I couldn't let her get to me. Five minutes of quality. This was my chance.

I avoided making eye contact, instead focusing my full attention on not tripping up the stairs. Once I'd conquered the steps, I paused and squinted at the crowd. The lights were too bright to see faces.

I was supposed to say my name first, then walk to center stage. I opened my mouth and . . .

My name.

My . . . name?

Um . . .

Wait, don't say um. Uh . . .

"We're ready when you are, Miss Bascomb."

27

Bascomb. That's right. And my first name is . . . Desi! Huzzah!

"My name is Desi Bascomb." I projected my voice as I strode to center stage. Then . . . I froze again. Come on, I thought. I've had harder acting jobs than this. These are high school students, not royalty. I fanned myself with my sheet. If I got through without passing out or flooding the stage with sweat, I could probably make Tree Number Two.

"I'm an eighth grader," I continued. "My favorite color is teal and I like gummy bears." I cleared my throat and looked down at my sheet, trying my best to ignore the fact that it was shaking. Or the fact that I'd had three Mountain Dews before this audition, and you can guess what I had to do. Or Dew.

I raised my hand to my heart and stared straight into the spotlight. After clearing my throat, I dove into the monologue.

"Call me fair? That fair again unsay.
Demetrius loves your fair: O happy fair!"

My voice came out squeaky, definitely not theatrical or Shakespearean. I wrapped my arms around my middle and looked away. I thought of the meaning behind the words. Helena liked the guy who was in love with her best friend. Here she was saying that she'd give anything to have Demetrius feel that love for her instead.

I knew that ache. There'd been my stupid crush on Hayden, and then the whole Karl-Elsa thing, which could be a Shakespearean play all by itself. If only there was a guy out

28

there who liked me as Just Desi. Someone who appreciated me in my own world.

I stared back into the spotlight. My whole body throbbed with Helena's angst. I tingled all over with emotion, almost to the point that I *was* Helena. It was the same sensation I felt when I connected to my princess clients, when my MP was tuned in. But magic only happened when I wore the Royal Rouge makeup. How could I have this magical feeling happen at home, away from Façade?

I spoke again, punctuating the monologue with my swelling energy.

"... *My ear should catch your voice, my eye your eye,*
My tongue should catch your tongue's sweet melody.
Were the world mine, Demetrius being bated,
The rest I'd give to be to you translated.
O! teach me how you look, and with what art
You sway the motion of Demetrius' heart."

A splattering of applause rang out in the theater—which had to be a good thing, right? I blinked, the magic of the words gone, and I was back to worrying about death by sweat.

"Um, no wait ... thank you." I curtsied, an old occupational hazard from subbing, and exited the stage. Reed gave me a nod, but I didn't sit down. Instead, I pushed open the theater door and retreated to the bathroom to undo the Dew.

I caught my reflection when I stepped out of the stall. My complexion was pale, but also kind of glowing. Who would have thought all those nerves could create such a rush? I lifted my arm to redo my ponytail and stopped. Ew . . . I may have had that golden Helena moment, but in the process, I'd also gotten sweaty. I swear I'd put on deodorant that morning. Stupid generic brand.

And . . . great. There was a huge smudge of chocolate near the bottom right hem of my shirt. Why hadn't I noticed that *before* I stood in front of the entire theater department? I hit the faucet and a gush of water squirted all over me. Sweat circles, chocolate, and a half-soaked shirt. Eighth-grade genius right here.

The shirt wasn't going to dry out on its own, and I still needed to go back in to watch the rest of the tryouts. A brainiac idea snuck in, but I brushed it away like a piece of lint. No, I couldn't. Well, I *could* . . .

Wet the whole T-shirt.

Seriously! Then it would look like I'd spilled soda and had to wash it off. A fully soaked shirt was far less embarrassing than the Sweat Circles of Doom and Choco Stain-o. I crouched close to the sink and hosed myself off. Kind of soothing, actually. When I was good and dripping, I punched the hand dryer to evaporate the drippiness, but it didn't start. I wasn't even attending this high school yet, and it was already messing with my head.

I shook my hands, and when I did, a bubble formed from the droplets of water. Instead of popping, it drifted up to the ceiling.

Wait . . .

Was it . . .

Growing? Oh yeah. The bubble morphed from water-melon size to beach ball to full capacity.

I nearly shouted *"Ta-da!"* when my princess agent, Meredith, stepped out.

"Darling." She leaned against the other sink, her nose scrunched in disgust. "I'm rather positive *A Midsummer Night's Dream* does not have a wet T-shirt contest in it."

"Meredith!" I covered my chest. "Why do you always pop up like that?"

"I travel by bubble. I find *popping* is a rather apropos entrance."

I finally realized what seeing my agent meant—work! Blessed work! I squealed and gave her a hug. "You're back! Does this mean I'm ready for Level Two? Did I get all my training in? Why didn't you tell me you were coming? Where are we going?"

She jerked out of my embrace. "Let's talk in the bubble. The fluorescents in this bathroom make my hair look limy. And your hair, well . . . just get in."

Chapter 4

The interior of Meredith's bubble was more fabulous than ever. Instead of the one office with a sitting area, she now had a reception room with a couch, TV, and a wet bar. A massive gift basket covered a coffee table. Her office, visible from behind the cracked door, had the same monochromatic color scheme as before, but with nicer bookcases, a glass-top desk, and a painting that I was pretty sure I'd seen in one of my art books. She pointed to her new hardwood floors. "Drip, drip, drip. Must you always return to me looking like a wet dog?"

"I had a sweat situation."

She sighed. "You *are* a situation."

"Hi, Desi!" I said sarcastically. "Welcome back to work. Sorry I didn't get you earlier but . . ."

"But"—Meredith handed me a towel and pointed to two chairs circling a chrome end table—"you weren't ready. Remember, Façade is about quality versus quantity at Level Two, so we don't like to rush. I gave you your BEST requirements and you've now completed them."

"I did? How?"

"Well, you barely scraped by with the music—let's hope all your classical research is enough since your violin playing sounded like—"

"Screaming cats. I know."

"Please. That's an insult to felines everywhere. I'll have to inflate your skills on the BEST report. And you just completed the public speaking task with your audition." Meredith tugged her low green ponytail tighter. "And don't dwell on this too long, but I think you did rather well."

"Really? I've gotta tell you, Meredith, it was so bizarre. Like, I was on that stage but also somewhere in England with Helena, you know? Remember when you told me that if I went Zen, I could really feel my MP? Well, I focused on Helena, and all these . . . these feelings came flooding in, and it didn't matter that I was talking all Shakespearey. I'm sure it makes no sense, but it felt like full-blown magic. I know subs need the Royal Rouge for magic to even happen, but maybe this was, I don't know, mini-magic?"

"Is this your scientific term? Mini-magic?"

"You didn't answer my question."

"You don't even know what you're talking about. And you've been here for two seconds and you're already grilling me." Meredith drew herself up to her full height, which couldn't have been more than five feet two, although her attitude took up a lot more space than that. "But I am happy to see you doing so well at home. I'm making an espresso. Do you want one?"

"Hot chocolate?"

"Beverage of the juvenile. Hold on."

She got to work making our drinks with her new fancy coffee machine. And although I managed to get hot chocolate on my shirt in five seconds, Meredith's gauzy white top and green linen pants stayed clean and pressed, just like her brown skin always looked airbrushed and her nails perfectly manicured and . . . Wait, linen pants? What happened to her power suit?

"So what's with all the changes?"

"Instant coffee is disgusting."

"Not that. The office. Your look."

"My look? Following the trends of the season, darling. And the office is a bonus. After you did so well at the Court of Royal Appeals, Genevieve decided all my previous privileges could be restored. Welcome to the Level Two treatment. Speaking of which, that gift basket is for you."

"Me? Can I open it?"

"That's usually what you do with gift baskets."

I rushed over to the tower of treats. The card inside read,

Desi,

We're so excited about your advancement.
Welcome to Level Two, darling.
Royally yours, The Façade Agency.

I untied the elaborate bow holding the cellophane together, and pushed back the tissue paper until I got to the goodies. And holy goodies: inside was high-end makeup, scented lotions, three cute tops, funky heels I would never dare walk in, gourmet chocolates, and a watch that was way too fancy for a teenage girl from Sproutville to ever pull off. I oohed and ahhed over each gift, still in shock that any of it was mine. "There has to be hundreds of dollars of stuff in here."

"Try thousands," Meredith said. "That watch alone is eight hundred."

I fingered the watch. My mom's Miss Idaho tiara didn't even cost that much. "But . . . this is the royal treatment. Why are they giving this to me? I'm just a sub."

"A *Level Two* sub. You're about to start a whole new ball game. You'll see how different things are when you get to your first job."

I smeared on some pink lip gloss. "And when is that going to be?"

"You'll get an in-depth report on it once you've gone through a quick Level Two initiation. You do feel ready to take on a higher-level princess, yes?"

"Yeah. Sure. Slap a job right on me." I smacked my

lips and reached for the box of chocolates. "I'm easy."

"No, you aren't easy. That's exactly what I wanted to talk to you about." Meredith set her cup on the saucer. "Although you did well enough in court, no more meddling in the princesses' lives, or kissy business, unless it is specifically noted in the princesses' profiles, which I sincerely doubt because most girls don't like subs kissing their prince."

Kissing their prince. Ah, Karl. Such a nice mouth. I rubbed my lip-glossed lips together. I wondered if I'd ever run into him on a job. It would be fun to see him. And his soft lips. Did I mention those?

"You're not answering. Darling." Meredith rubbed her temples. "If we get some time in between gigs, I'll take you around town and introduce you to a nice Parisian boy. They're far more entertaining and *real*. I'm sure our cover agency, Mirage, has a cute male model they can spare."

I pushed away my Karl thoughts and pasted on what I hoped was a professional expression. "Meredith. It's fine. I'm too young for all of that anyway."

"Really?" She snorted. "Because I saw you buying a certain magazine the other day, and I'm guessing it wasn't for the 'Ten Steps to Better Thighs' article."

I almost choked on my anger. "Don't you have better things to do than run surveillance on my grocery shopping? Yes, okay, so I might have had a tiny, fleeting crush, but I let it go. Just like you did with your prince, right?"

It was a low blow. When I'd last seen her, Meredith had

written a text to the very prince whom she'd dumped after a nearly career-crushing relationship during her days as a sub. It must have been years since they'd last been in touch. True love or not, Façade employees dating royals is way taboo. I had no idea what became of that text, but this wasn't a secret she would ever want exposed.

We stared at each other before Meredith dropped her gaze. Point to Desi.

"Yes. Exactly," she said. "Now, Miss Professional, if you'll step out of the bubble, we can get your Level Two initiation done."

"We're here? But . . ."

"I wish I could say I've missed your endless questioning, but insincerity makes me itch. Yes. We're here. Smoother landing and improved parking privileges are all part of the upgrade. Leave your gift basket here, and I'll make sure you get it back later. If you think that makeup in there is a hint, then you're right. Would mascara really hurt?"

"You sound like my mother." I squeezed through the bubble wall. I didn't need mascara when I was just going to look like someone else soon anyway. And by someone, I meant an important, cultured, Level Two princess.

Once we were in the lobby of Façade, the bubble floated back into Meredith's remote. She gave the gadget a squeeze of affection. "I so love my ride."

And I so loved the regal grandeur of Façade. The reception area glowed from the sunlight reflecting through the stained-glass windows. Museum curators would salivate if they knew about the collection of priceless royal artifacts—from golden toothbrushes to a marbled baptismal font—neatly displayed throughout the vast hall. But the artist creating a Façade tile mosaic behind the reception desk was new. So were the tables being set up near the tiara wall. Anticipation hummed in every corner.

"What's going on here?" I asked.

"Genevieve's seventieth birthday is this month, and we're renovating for the event. Everything needs to be perfect so we can show Specter who is king. Or queen, rather."

"Who is Specter? Is he on the council?"

"Specter isn't a person. It's another branch of the agency, a bit of a rival, actually."

"What do they do?"

"Less than they claim." Meredith waved her hand. "It's difficult to keep track of all the divisions and their responsibilities. Actually, the big news is Genevieve may be announcing her retirement, and if that happens, the whole council will be reorganized. Promotions will be in store."

"You think *you're* getting a promotion? Please."

Meredith and I both cringed at the voice. We exhaled in unison and turned around to face Lilith, Meredith's long-time adversary, who was perched on the waiting area couch, sewing a quilt. Long fingers dipped the needle in and out of the fabric. Her domestic goddess look was punctuated by a pressed floral halter dress. Gah, she even had on pearls.

Meredith smoothed out her shirt and sat across from Lilith on a wing chair. Instead of taking a seat, I stood and let them have their space. Their expressions were so hard, I half expected a bikini-clad woman to parade by with a round-one sign like at boxing matches. Right before the fight bell rings.

"Did I give you a tour of my new bubble, Lilith?" Meredith raised an eyebrow. "It's a model NT-94. I think you're still in a JD-35, yes?"

Lilith busied herself with her sewing, the design a multi-colored tree. "Bubble models matter little compared to cold, hard numbers. As commoners say, my promotion is in the bag. And yours, well, more likely in the trash."

"Careful, darling. Arrogance will make that little wrinkle on your forehead grow."

"Please. Your chances of moving out of mid-list obscurity are about as good as that prince of yours proposing."

Meredith's smile tightened. I sucked in a breath. I was not a Lilith fan, but I had to hand it to her—she knew where to strike.

"That prince," Meredith said evenly, "is my past. If we're bringing him up, why don't we also mention that you were the one who shared all the details with the council, the details I told you in confidence *as a friend*. Backstabbing doesn't seem like a trait that would get you on the council, now, does it?"

Whoa. Lilith was the snitch? More surprising—they used to be friends? I needed to get my manual out and take notes. Juicy, juicy stuff.

"It's business, Mer." Lilith bit neatly on a thread. "You

have to know the rules and where you fit. See this quilt I'm making for Genevieve's birthday? It's her family tree."

She held it out for Meredith to take in the details. Meredith tried to act uninterested, but her eyes kept drawing back to the design. Carefully stitched names and dates wove up the branches.

"Four of her family branches have royal bloodlines." Lilith pointed to a branch. "Four! It's almost enough to earn her a title."

"What's your point?" Meredith asked.

"Our reputations aren't our only defining traits. Sure, you can sit around patting your back because of all your do-gooding, but it doesn't change where you came from. If I were making a family tree for you, it'd be nothing more than a stump."

"Pedigree stopped mattering two hundred years ago. Royals don't even care about bloodlines anymore—the Crown Prince of Norway met his wife at a rock concert, for heaven's sake," Meredith said.

Lilith leaned over and patted Meredith's knee. I could tell it took all of my agent's self control to not kick Lilith in the face.

"Of course he did, dear." She lowered her voice. "But to put it bluntly, the agency wants to know we're devoted to these clients, and being cut from the same cloth makes it that much easier to assimilate into royal roles. I had two counts and a duchess at my boarding school. These people were in my circle before I even knew about Façade."

"Assimilate? I went through five foster homes. Don't tell me I don't know how to *assimilate*."

"No hard feelings." Lilith shrugged and folded up the blanket. "When I move up, I'll make sure you get more of those Level One surrogates you're so fond of."

I hated when Lilith called substitutes *surrogates*.

"Ahem, Level Two right here," I said, regretting it as soon as I spoke. Their attention shifted to me, the informative feud over.

Lilith sniffed. "Did you forget to wipe you shoes before you stepped out of the bubble, Meredith? Smells like . . . Idaho."

I pursed my lips into a smile. Lilith had charmed me during my Level One training, but now I saw how deceitful and condescending she was. So, yeah, she did kind of own the whole lavender-and-lace look, but she was a total snob. Seriously, Scarlett O'Hara in *Gone with the Wind* was a sweetheart next to her. "Hi, Lilith."

"Oh, Desi dear!" Lilith gave me the once-over. "I didn't even *notice* you."

Meredith stood. "Well, we couldn't help but notice you, darling. Your fragrance is so cheap, how could we not?"

"This is from the Façade boutique." Lilith looked down at her wrist. "I like to support this agency any way I can."

"Like perfume is supportive," I said.

"Spoken like a non-deserving, uneducated Level Two." Lilith rolled her eyes. "You probably can't even apply eyeliner."

I snorted. "Eyeliner has nothing to do with being a good sub."

Meredith squeezed my elbow. "She's right. You're digging a hole. Let me talk, okay?"

I opened my mouth. Meredith loathed Lilith. Why would she agree with her, and of all times, during a makeup argument?

"Lilith, you can sit around knitting blankets, clinging to your family's rotting tree, while I'm going to go get some actual work done. Promotion is mine, darling. Game. On." Meredith pivoted on her heel and marched toward one of the hallways attached to the circular lobby. Lilith smirked at me one more time. I did the mature thing and avoided sticking out my tongue. I couldn't resist a parting line, though. I pointed at her blanket and said, "Your stitches are sloppy."

So maybe I'd have to check the manual and see if there was a section on better insults. Regardless, I held my chin high as I hurried past the tiara wall to where Meredith waited on a velvet bench. She patted the spot next to her.

"Sorry I lost my cool. That woman gets under my skin."

"Yeah, well, *her* skin has scales underneath it."

Meredith snickered. Where was that line when I'd said the stupid stitches thing?

"What was that all about anyway?" I asked. "I know Lilith is vicious, but you two seemed like you were out for blood."

"Ever since the news broke that Genevieve might be retiring, the whole agency has been on edge. When the Head of Council leaves, everything is restructured. Someone from the court will become the new head. That court member must then be replaced, so all the agents and coordinators of various divisions start vying for the seat on court. And when you start dangling promotions in front of a very ambitious group of employees, most who have MP, well . . . Façade will be unstable for a while."

"Wait, so . . . divisions. Are there six, one for each member of the court?"

"There are dozens of divisions that I know of, more probably that I don't. The court members are assigned two or three each, and Genevieve manages the main branches, like Central Command, Specter, and our subbing branch, which is actually called Glimmer."

"I've never heard our division called that."

"I avoid the word myself. Too sparkly. There's also Bubble Maintenance, Mirage, Glamourification, Historical Preservation, Human Resources . . . I can't list them all."

"I don't know about of *half* of those. Tell me about them! This is so cool."

"Not now. Genevieve is the only one who knows how far-reaching the agency goes, and that's because she's the only one who *needs* to know. All you need to worry about right now is your own job. So hush about it. She'll be here soon."

"Who? Genevieve?"

Meredith ignored me, pulling out her remote and punching random buttons. Of course I had a million more questions to ask, but I could tell Meredith was already worked up.

She would have to be to call the agency "unstable." Looking around at the stone walls, I had never seen anything more solid in my life.

A few minutes passed before Genevieve rounded the corner. I had known she was important before, but now that Meredith told me *how* important, the sight of her caused me to sit up straighter. Genevieve's rainbow hair was perfectly curled, and her wizened brown eyes crinkled when she smiled. She looked like a modern-day Mrs. Claus in her red business suit. Mrs. Claus, if she ditched Santa, dyed her hair, and took on the most powerful job in the world.

She held out her arms. "Thank you for waiting. So sorry I wasn't here sooner."

Meredith stood and air kissed Genevieve. Next, Genevieve turned to me and gave me a delicate hug, her vanilla-and-cinnamon scent clinging to me long after she'd let go. "Desi. Welcome back. Did you have a nice break? Anything exciting in . . . is it Montana?"

"Idaho." I glanced at Meredith to make sure it was all right to correct someone so much higher up. "And I just started school a few weeks back."

"Oh, how fun! I always loved my adolescent studies. Although, BEST proved to be as essential. And since you're here, you've obviously completed your tasks for your next client, yes?"

I nodded.

"Then that will allow us to focus on you today and what your skills are as a sub."

"Oh, so you're doing the initiation today? I'm . . . I'm honored."

"I take all our Level Twos to Dorshire Hall," Genevieve said. "It's one of my favorite traditions at Façade."

"Thank you. Are you sure you're not too busy?"

"Time. Pish." Genevieve patted my hand. "You forget, we have all the time in the world. Little company perk. The Law of Duplicity means we don't age as quickly."

The Law of Duplicity was Façade's version of time travel. I didn't understand the science (or magic) behind the law, but Façade was able to magically manipulate time so that my home life practically stood still while I was away subbing. When I came home, time played out like I had been in two places at once. Sometimes my return was a second or two off, but otherwise . . . Blows my mind. "So the bubble traveling makes you age slower?"

"Seemingly, yes. The right skin creams also help."

"Well, I'll be going, then," Meredith said. "You're in for an absolute treat, Desi. Dorshire Hall is one of a kind. Meet me over in the Glamourification Studio when you're done—it's across from Central Command."

Genevieve looped her arm through mine and led me up a small staircase as Meredith hurried in another direction. "Now, Dorshire privileges are extended to high-level agents and council members, but we make a special exception for our subs when they start a new level. I like to get to know my girls. A thank-you for working so hard at Façade."

Two French doors opened when we reached the top of

the staircase. A graying man shaped like a sideways football bowed and cleared his throat. "Your table is ready, Madame Genevieve." He then turned to me and appraised my still-damp SHAKESPEARE ROCKETH shirt and jeans. "I see your guest will need to be properly attired."

"Please, Bosworth," Genevieve said.

Bosworth bowed again and swept his hand for us to enter. The reception area was dark with wood walls. Immediately to the right was a coat closest.

No, a *dress* closest.

There were hundreds of dresses in every size and fashion. Bosworth motioned with his nose to a rack. "Your size, I presume. Pick what you like."

Meredith wasn't kidding. Level Two was packed with perks.

Chapter 5

I rummaged through the racks and came out with a simple black boatneck dress that looked just like the one Audrey Hepburn wore in *Breakfast at Tiffany's*. Genevieve nodded her approval. "Bosworth will provide you with shoes. You may change and meet me at our table."

At the end of the closet was a small dressing room. I slipped out of my clothes and into the dress, which fit me better than anything I'd ever worn. And it was dry.

I stepped out of the dressing space and was promptly handed some gold ballet slippers and a quilted tote bag from Bosworth. "For the lady's . . . attire."

"Thank you, Bosworth. Can I call you Bos?"

"The lady may follow me."

I shoved my T-shirt and jeans into the bag and followed Bos past the small entry to the sun-drenched dining area.

The regal excess of this job was to be expected, but even the richest of royals would have been impressed with the majestic glow of Dorshire Hall. Antique tables dotted the vast room, wallpapered in a lush cream damask. Seemingly every monarchy, past and present, was represented through delicate china, polished silverware, or priceless furniture. Pictures of hundreds of royals covered every inch of the vaulted ceilings, sloping high into a watchful V. We reached our table and Bosworth pulled out my seat.

So this was Level Two. *This* I could get used to.

Genevieve smiled at me from behind her teacup. "Bringing a sub here for the first time is one of my favorite parts of the job. Now, don't worry about what to order; the chef's five courses are preset."

"This is amazing." I swigged my ice water and scanned the room. "This is all . . . amazing. You probably hear this all the time, but I feel like a princess."

"It is lovely, isn't it?" She appraised the room. "Now, let's get down to business. Before we discuss you, Desi, I want you to look at the portraits above us. How do you feel?"

"Uh . . . overwhelmed. And honored. To be in their presence. They're all royal, right?"

"Not all of them. Dorshire Hall chronicles Façade's history as well. You see the mother of our agency, Woserit, right there." She pointed to a painting done in profile of a woman with dark skin and black-lined eyes, dressed in ancient Egyptian robes. "You remember Woserit discovered that the silt in the Nile had transformative properties. By disguising herself to protect her queen, she became the first substitute.

"After discovering that magic, Woserit passed down the secret of the silt we use in the rouge to her female descendants. For generations and generations, no one beyond her lineage was aware of the magic she'd unearthed."

I stared at the portraits twisting up the walls. "So where did Façade come from if Woserit's family was the only one that knew about the magic?"

Genevieve indicated another painting, this one of a woman with a sly smile, wearing a medieval headdress. She was posed next to a hunting dog. "That's Beatrix the Bold. Beatrix was the first of Woserit's descendants to explore the silt's components. She found that the silt only worked on those with a sort of magical potential, what we now call MP. That led her to define and conduct tests on MP—who had it, what caused it. As you know, a human's dormant MP ignites when it interacts with another organism."

"Mine was fish," I said, thinking back to the day I'd made a wish on the fish in the back of the pet store. I'd wanted to be a girl who made an impact, and now with this job, well . . . wish granted.

"Yes, I had a rather frightening run-in with a rhinoceros, but it proved to be for the best. Beatrix believed her MP was sparked by her dog. MP is unique to each individual, not hereditary, although Woserit's magical descendants are *highly* valued at Façade." Meredith took another sip of tea. "Beatrix was also an early scientist and inventor. She actually made our first bubble—nearly died flying it."

"Busy woman." I stared up at Beatrix's calculated gaze.

"Shrewd woman. She knew that magical power should be limited, that if it was discovered, it could be used for evil. So she made a secret pact with world leaders—magic would be used solely on royals. In exchange, they promised to fund the newly founded Façade agency. We've followed her business model ever since."

"But she gave power to the already powerful. And lots of monarchs are evil."

Genevieve leaned back as our first course—a lovely cheese-and-fruit platter—was presented. "That's partially why she made the pact. The royals have no access to the magic beyond what we provide for them. By agreeing to that limit, we hold the power, not them."

"And what power is that, exactly?"

"Ah, that is what we need to discuss. MP. Now, subs can only use their magic while wearing Royal Rouge, but your performance can be amplified if you tap into your MP. Often, there is a particular emotion or character trait—unique to each person—which allows you to feel your magic more strongly. When you channel your triggering emotion, your capabilities for Façade increase. It takes years of subbing before you'll even sense it."

"You mean, like a buzzy feeling?"

Genevieve looked surprised. "It can be different for everyone, but that's one way to describe it. When did you notice this sensation?"

"Well, Meredith said I could use my emotions as a way to get through a confusing job. So I felt the buzzing when I was . . . uh, I call it impacting the princesses." I nibbled on a strawberry. "It's most intense when I'm trying to make a choice, deciding what my clients would want, kind of feeling their drama for them. Gets pretty intense."

"Interesting." Genevieve tapped her lips with her finger. "Play with that more. Figure out what those moments most have in common. We call it magic potential for a reason—the more you learn to tune into it, the stronger your power becomes."

"I've never thought of it as a power."

"Then start. It's important that you're aware. Which is why we have these discussions. Your superiors should be informed concerning your experiences—lets us know how best to help you and our clients."

"Well, something weird happened earlier today." I pushed my plate to the side and scooted in. "Okay. I was trying out for my school play and I felt that same buzzy feeling when I was getting into character. For the role of Helena. So I thought of her like I do the princesses, really tried to imagine—"

"Well, that's different." Genevieve made an odd face, like I'd dug in to my food with my bare hands. "You can't use your magic apart from Façade purposes, of course. MP is merely the potential for magic. Without our monitoring, without the rouge, you have no capabilities."

"But I don't understand why it would feel the same."

Genevieve patted my hand. "Emotions can be hard to decipher. Perhaps you were extremely nervous."

"When I'm nervous, I get sick. This was more like the time I decided Elsa liked Karl, so I kissed—"

"It's probably best we don't discuss that particular incident, my dear." Genevieve smiled kindly. "Oh, Chef's second course is coming. I adore his cranberry salad."

My face flushed with heat. Brilliant—mentioning to the Head of Council the act that almost got me kicked out of the agency. I hadn't meant to bring it up, I was just trying to explain all the bizarre feelings I'd been having. I was beyond relieved when Genevieve asked, "Did I mention this china is over a hundred years old? Late Qing dynasty, I believe. Excellent workmanship."

And then the moment was over and Genevieve continued on, sharing details about the room, stories from her subbing days. The rest of the food was served, course after course, until I began to wish I'd opted for a nice toga instead of the formfitting dress.

"I don't think I've seen a sub eat like that since I brought Meredith in here," said Genevieve, after dessert.

"Sorry!" I swallowed. "Was that bad manners? The food was delicious."

"No apology necessary. My plate is clean as well."

"So. Meredith. What was she like as a sub?" I asked.

"We've had hundreds of girls come through here. I don't remember them all. But I do remember Meredith." Genevieve dabbed at her mouth with a napkin. "Despite some of her later choices regarding a certain prince, Meredith has always been dedicated to this agency. She's an extremely hard worker and very aware and in control of her MP. She's a wonderful example for you."

"Yeah. Except I probably wouldn't go with the chartreuse hair."

"I see you more with a nice teal." Genevieve glanced at her diamond watch and rose to her feet. "Speaking of, you need to meet Meredith in the Glamourification Studio. I hope you enjoyed our meal and chat."

"Yes. Thank you." I stumbled up. "You went all out."

"You're special, Desi. If nothing else, remember that. Subs are rare breeds, and we value your abilities a great deal. Without MP, we wouldn't be in business. Now, as I'm sure Meredith told you, my dreaded birthday approaches and I must attend to some details. Best of luck with your Level Two adventures. I'm sure you'll be a star."

She leaned in for an air kiss, but I moved in the same direction and ended up kissing her hair. My skills in fancydom were going to need some serious work.

Bosworth escorted me back to the hallway, telling me to keep the dress and to maybe "use it as inspiration for further wardrobe adjustments."

I realized once I was back down the staircase that I hadn't asked Genevieve where, or even *what*, the Glamourification

Studio was. I hadn't seen anyone who could point me in the right direction. Maybe I should go back and ask peppy Bosworth.

Except . . . wait. This was the first time I'd been inside Façade without anyone hurrying me around. And since I didn't have an escort, I could get a little "lost."

I took my time wandering down the hallways, reading the placards on the artifacts that lined the walls. Suits of armor stood at attention as I fingered swords and royal crests. Every door I passed was a different size and color, giving me the feeling that I'd jumped down Alice's rabbit hole. I didn't dare open them—I was curious, not stupid—but then I came to an open doorway with FAÇADE TRAVEL etched on the glass. Open door = open invitation.

Inside was a single room with a small, empty desk in the corner. Pictures of tropical locations covered the walls with signs above reading LUXURY! and RELAX! In the center of the room were two thin couches and a model of a grandiose hotel.

I knelt down next to the model. Twelve smaller, private cabanas circled the larger structure, which enclosed a pool complete with rock slides and hidden grottos. A stack of brochures were fanned out on a table next to the model. I picked one up and read:

THE FAÇADE RESORT: *Our exclusive royal retreat.*

It was an answer to a question I'd never thought to ask. *This is where the royals vacation when they use a sub.*

It made perfect sense. You can't let a princess ski the Alps looking like herself while her sub was back home pretending to be royal. So they were all sent to one place. And that place was . . .

Nestled in the southwest corner of the Bermuda Triangle, the Façade Resort is so exclusive, no one besides our clients even know it exists. You'll get the royal treatment in your private cabana.

Façade had thought of everything. I snuck out of the room and tried to retrace my steps back to the main lobby, finally coming to a somewhat familiar hallway. There was Central Command, the place I'd first gotten my manual. Directly across was a bright pink door that I assumed was the Glamourification Studio. I knocked, and when no one answered, pushed my way in, sucking in my breath when I realized Meredith had been right about the Lilith comment: makeup here was a much bigger deal than I could have possibly imagined.

Chapter
6

The room's mirrored walls made it very unclear where anything began or ended. And even without the reflections, I imagined the effect would be the same, because the shelves of makeup wound endlessly around the glittering space. The color came mostly from the makeup itself, all organized by product—creams for every skin color, polishes in purples, metallics, and reds. Crystal bottles of perfume caught the warm, subdued lighting. Women in head-to-toe black, all with pink hair cut into blunt bobs, hustled around the counters.

One of these girls dabbed foundation on Meredith's forehead. Meredith snapped her fingers and the employee supplied a compact. My feet sank into the shag carpet as

I crossed over to my agent, who saw my reflection in her mirror. She turned around and beamed.

"I love showing my subs this place. I won a trip to Bloomingdale's in New York when I was eight, and it didn't even begin to compare to this."

The idea that Meredith had ever been eight, or had childhood memories, was too weird to consider.

"So," Meredith said, "are you going to say anything, or are you too awestruck?"

"When Lilith mentioned eyeliner, I had no clue you guys took this stuff so . . . seriously."

Meredith laughed. "We make a quarter of our revenue here. This isn't your average makeup. There is a reason some royals look particularly put together and others are, well"—she shuddered—"a prime example of what generations of keeping a tight bloodline will do to you."

She motioned to the woman behind the counter, who brought out a basic makeup kit consisting of four shades of eye shadow, one blush, two tubes of lipstick, and some loose powder. Meredith pointed at it. "This starter kit would put you back about fifty thousand U.S. dollars."

I sputtered. "For MAKEUP?"

"For eye shadow that never wears off until you want it to, powder that fills in every crease and pore, and blush that makes you look like your natural glow comes from inside. It all has a touch, just a touch, of the Egyptian silt we use in the rouge."

"So you *do* use magic on other stuff. You use it on makeup?"

Meredith shut the case. "We use it for the same purpose we use the rouge and bubbles and subs and everything else. To make the royals happy. And when royals are happy, they pay."

"So it's about money."

"You can't hand out a commodity like magic for free. Façade is a business. Its purpose certainly isn't about spreading good cheer. But they do include the starter kit in our agent's benefit package, along with our hair dye of choice. I'd say that's rather charitable."

I looked around the room some more. In the far back was a more antique counter. Rich mahogany, vintage powder puffs, scrolling details. Total glamour. "What's that?" I wove around the other displays.

Meredith followed and pointed to a sign written in cursive. "That's our Hollywood line. Most expensive products we have."

I picked up a bottle of *Some Like It Hot* nail polish. "This is great! It's like, the perfect red."

"I prefer Swan Princess Pink."

"You like Grace Kelly?"

"*High Society* is my favorite old movie." Meredith sighed. "Witty banter, a love triangle, snappy music. Plus, Frank Sinatra is an absolute dreamboat."

I set the makeup down. Did Meredith—*Meredith*—just say *dreamboat*? "So where do they make this makeup?"

Meredith pointed to a door in the corner. "In our lab. They're geniuses in there. The newest creation is a serum that keeps you frizz-free for weeks."

"Do they test out anything besides makeup?"

Meredith shrugged. "I'm an agent. And you're a sub. It's not our division, and thus not our concern. What we *do* need to worry about is getting you briefed for your first Level Two gig. You'll have more material to go over now, so I want to make sure you get enough time. To the bubble!"

Once we'd made it back to the main lobby and safely into her bubble, Meredith sat me down. "I need to make some phone calls. We're not traveling far, so I'm setting the bubble to hover until you're fully briefed."

I waited until she'd slipped into her office before leaning back in the chair and staring at her ceiling. Crown moldings . . . that's new. Crown molding? Who cares about that—I'd just had the most glamorous day of my life! Was I ever going to get used to this? I had, after all, worked here before, yet every time I learned something else, it felt like I knew nothing at all. How far and wide did the abilities of my employer stretch?

At least the princess profile was in a familiar format:

PRINCESS MILLIE (Mildred. But who wants to be called Mildred?)

Age: 13

Hometown: Leichemburg (Although I'm doing a tour of Europe with Auntie Oksana right now, and it's been a longggg trip.)

Favorite Book: *War and Peace.* I haven't read it. I just like how thick it is.

Favorite Food: French vanilla cupcakes with purple sprinkles

Anything Else We Should Know: Hi! I'm Millie. You've probably heard of me before—not that I'm bragging, but I'm royalty and I figure with the job you have, you know about all of us, right? So sorry if some of this is review for you. . . . You're only my second sub. I turned thirteen two months ago, and it couldn't have come at a better time, believe me.

I'm supposed to go to this art exhibit thingy with my great-aunt Oksana, the Duchess of Leichemburg. Social events to her are always a super big deal, so I'm sure she'd KILL me if she knew I was using a sub. I need you to be really, really good, okay?

Now, the exhibit itself is going to be cool. It's a costume party, so I had an adorable dress made—you're welcome! I'm kinda sad I'm missing it, actually, but then I found out that the Earl of Nortenberg is bringing his son, and I about DIED. See, two years ago, at boarding school, I got in a fight with this girl named Lynette, who thinks she's better than me just because her dad owns an island. Hello! Ninth in line to rule my country over here.

Anyway, she pulled this nasty prank where she told Lord Gavin that I LIKE HIM. I don't know if you know Gavin, but he is not my type. At all. So as if it's not embarrassing enough to have a guy I don't even care about thinking that I have a crush on him, then he goes around telling everyone that:

A. I'm in love with him.

B. He totally doesn't like me.

C. I'm trying to use my family connections to
    get him to date me.

It was, to say the least, the worst thing that could ever
happen EVER. I begged my parents to let me take a term
off and travel with Auntie Oksana, at least until this blew
over. I also promised myself I would never talk to that jerk
again. EVER.

So I need you to do two things. First, be me. I
mean, as me as you can be so that my aunt doesn't get
suspicious. Because she will. The woman can spot a cubic
zirconium tiara from across the room and I'm sure she's
way familiar with Façade. I've added enough here so you
can get an idea of who I am. Please read and remember it
all. Also, don't talk to Gavin if you see him. Like, don't say
a word! He doesn't deserve the satisfaction. You can nod, I
guess. Maybe grunt. But, really, just stay away.

Okay now, they gave me this application thingy to fill
out, but I'm not sure it covers everything. So I made some
notes for you. I figure you'll be glad—the more you know,
the better, right?

There was twenty pages of everything, and I mean *every-thing*, that I would ever need to know about Millie. Her school, her friend's names, her family history, the music she played at her last violin concert, how she liked her toast buttered . . .

The Level One princesses had provided simple fact

sheets that had done little to prepare me for their situations. This was the opposite—there was so much information it was hard to decide what was relevant, although I could see how the BEST would help on the job. The manual had a highlighting feature, and I went through the letter and underlined all the important points. I'd have my manual with me if I needed to know how Millie liked her meat (medium-well—no pink in the middle!) or her uncles' names (Hanover, Ulysses, and . . . Greg? No, Craig).

After an hour of memorizing Millie's favorite shoe designers, I'd stored everything I possibly could. Then I looked her up on the chat rooms and was hit with a new wave of details and facts.

But it didn't take learning her favorite zoo animal to understand the message: Don't change anything. In my previous jobs, I'd tried to figure out the princess's hidden wishes, and then fulfilled them. Millie, however, didn't want me to stand up to her sister or land her a boyfriend. On the contrary: she wanted me to be as Millie as possible, right down to her beverage choice.

I got out my Royal Rouge compact, smiling at my reflection. Fatigue and pages of memorization was so much better than being clueless. This job would be more what I'd initially pictured subbing to be—a long event with important people. Like in *Roman Holiday*, where Audrey Hepburn plays a princess so tired from standing in a reception line that she takes off her shoe under her dress and nearly falls. Funny, but not catastrophic.

I stood and stretched, calling Meredith's name but stopping mid-word when I saw that her door was slightly open. The temptation to eavesdrop was too great. I crossed the room in silence, standing just close enough to hear her muffled voice.

"—sub will be gone in a few minutes. I have another drop-off in an hour, so . . . I don't know. I might have some time."

She giggled. Her voice lowered and I couldn't hear anything else. Then, after more laughter, her voice rose. "You know I do. I'm just trying to make this work. Ah, you're cute when you're needy. Sure . . . okay . . . talk soon."

I bolted over to the couch and grabbed my manual, forcing a look of boredom onto my face. So Meredith *was* talking to her prince again! I knew it was a possibility but . . . how did she swing it? That must be why she was less edgy. I definitely supported anything that promoted Meredith Zen.

Meredith opened her door and cleared her throat. "Did you say something?"

"What?" I looked up from my manual. "Oh, yeah, I'm about done here."

"Great." She punched a button on her remote, and the bubble hummed. "Sorry, I had a confidential phone call."

I hid a smile. "No worries."

"Are you all read up? Rouged up?" she asked.

"Put on my Rouge a few minutes ago. I should be Milliefied in a bit."

"Go ahead, I know you probably have loads of questions."

"Actually, I think I'm good."

Meredith touched my forehead. "Really? Are you feeling all right? Is that you in there?"

"Funny."

"Well, darling, out you go, then."

"But you just started the bubble."

"We didn't have far to travel. And if you get a chance, do stop by and see the *Mona Lisa*. She used to work for the agency; hence the secret smile."

I stepped out into the night, onto a shining wet street facing a large glass pyramid surrounded by a breathtakingly prodigious fortress. I'd seen this place in enough movies to know where I was. The Louvre. Millie's "art exhibit thingy" was at the Louvre in Paris.

Meredith wasn't kidding. I hadn't traveled far from Façade's headquarters, but, man. I was a world away from Sproutville.

Chapter

7

I paused outside the translucent structure, watching myself transform.

Millie was short and scrawny, but her fingers had the long elegance of a violin player's. My little black dress became a powder-blue period piece, tight around my chest and waist, flowing down in yards and yards of fabric. No, tight isn't the word. Restrictive. Stifling. With each breath I took, I could feel the bodice cut into my ribs.

Agh, I had a corset on! Who wears corsets, even for a costume? Not to mention the lace. Oh wow, was there lace. I patted my hair—a wig arranged in a white powdered updo. No tiara on top, though. I still hadn't been able to wear one of those yet.

I never thought I'd be grateful for the one pageant prep workshop Mom had made me do with Celeste. We'd put on six-inch heels and too-tight dresses and teetered back and forth across the room until our feet blistered. Mom claimed walking with poise in those outfits could prepare us for anything. And it was true—even in this corseted poof factory, I was able to glide into the top of the see-through pyramid, which was empty except for two security guards. One nodded at me. "Did you get that fresh air you needed, Your Highness?"

Clever, Millie. "I did. I don't know how my ancestors ever dealt with corsets!"

"Your aunt is waiting for you at the bottom of the staircase."

My head wobbled from the wig's weight as I descended the spiral stairs. The expansive lobby was quiet and softly lit, although music and voices drifted from the Sully Wing. An old woman stood at the base of the winding stairs, her chin high and her patience low.

She wore red lipstick and a frown that made her millions of wrinkles sag even more. Her features, which at one time had no doubt been striking, were now sharp and birdlike. The feathers shooting out of her white wig only added to the fowl motif. Auntie Ostrich. But her brown eyes were intelligent and bright. They narrowed at me. "Millie. I do not like to be kept waiting."

"Sorry, Auntie Oksana."

"Tell your country you are sorry. It is them you are representing every minute you exist."

66

Her accent was subtle—refined and precise. I immediately rolled my shoulders back when she spoke. "Yes. Of course."

Auntie Ostrich leaned on my arm as we walked into the exhibition hall. Music from a string quartet drifted in, playing Bach's Minuet in G Major. I personally preferred Handel, but Bach did have some skills . . . Hey! Look at that. All those hours listening to classical music came in handy after all. I hoped my knowledge wouldn't need to stretch beyond recognition to actually playing. Having pyramid glass rain down on the partygoers due to my violin skills would not look good on a Princess Progress Report.

The guests matched our period-style costumes. I knew from my studies that the style was eighteenth-century baroque, probably around the time of Marie Antoinette. The monstrous cake on the dessert table confirmed my guess—a nod to the Marie Antoinette misquote, "Let them eat cake." Which was odd—we were in Paris, after all, where the French Revolution took place. Why have a party here with royals in attendance, celebrating a time when they *did away* with royals?

A man approached Auntie Ostrich and gave her a fluttery bow. "Thank you so much for coming, Your Highness. Have you had a chance to see the exhibit?"

"We've just arrived. Millie, this is the painter, Christian Mercier."

I dipped my head. Not a bow—I was the royal, after all.

"It would be an honor to show you my work personally, Your Highness," Christian said.

"As you wish."

We followed Christian past socialites sipping champagne. His paintings were hanging in a dark room with red lights illuminating each one. The pieces bore a stark similarity—red shapes and lines slashed onto white canvas, all dwarfed by boisterous gold frames (baroque style—go, me!).

Auntie Ostrich plucked cat-eye glasses from her clutch and peered at the paintings. "Yes, I see the juxtaposition you were going for. Wonderful hue you chose—something more rich would have been vulgar. The message comes off vaguely forced, though."

Christian's face reddened. "That was intended, Your Highness."

"Hmmm." Auntie Ostrich cast me a glance. "Millie, what do you think?"

My heart jumped. This was where all my studying and training came into play. Anyone can walk around in a ball gown, especially when that ball gown was the result of the Royal Rouge. Now I needed to remember everything I'd learned over the summer and add that to the information Millie provided for me.

I studied the paintings. The frames were a symbol of the extravagance of King Louis XVI's reign, and encased the much bleaker artwork, which symbolized . . . rage? Simplicity of the common man? Er . . . freedom? I could say any of these things and sound smart enough. But Millie didn't strike me as the type to dig up art metaphors, regardless of the top-notch education she'd received. Plus, I knew her aunt made her nervous (how couldn't she—Auntie Ostrich was going to peck me any second), so even in her best moment, Millie wouldn't come up with any of those ideas.

Millie had written something else, though: right between her ring size and the secret confession that she hated oranges—her favorite shape was a circle.

"I think you're right about the shade. If it was pinker, it would take away . . . the meaning of the piece. And I like the circles in that one." I pointed to the painting on the end. "It makes me feel . . . It makes me feel," I ended lamely.

Auntie Ostrich gave me a long stare before turning to Christian. "I agree. Pink would have been a disaster. I'd like to purchase the one with the circles for my niece, along with the one with the mid-line slash. The vertical one, not horizontal, of course."

"Wonderful." Christian glowed. "I'll let the curator know. Of course, it means far more to me that the pieces spoke to you. If you'll excuse me, I see my wife has arrived. She'll want to meet you both. Thank you, Your Highness."

Christian scurried away. I wanted to pump my fist in the air. My first Level Two obstacle equaled success!

Auntie Ostrich rubbed her arthritic knuckles. "I'll put my painting in the east wing. Third hallway . . . will complement the Degas I have there."

"Thank you for the painting," I said.

Auntie Ostrich began hobbling away from the exhibition, back to the festivities. "I've told you many times, it's important to begin your collection early—this piece will speak to you in a different way when you are older. I've always found that to be a wonder."

"Yes."

"You're rather quiet this evening."

Oops. The nerve-racking art discussion made me forget something vital about Millie: based on her bio, the girl probably spoke a mile a minute. I offered a feeble smile. "It's this corset. I'm sorry."

"I prefer it. Your usual prattling grates on me. But see to it that you engage in appropriate conversation with the guests. A tight corset hardly stopped your ancestors. You can start by thanking the Earl of Nortenberg and his son, Gavin. His wife sent us a lovely crystal vase from, I believe, the nineteenth century."

Wait. Red alert. Red alert. I had two jobs here—one was to be as Millie-like as possible so Auntie Ostrich didn't get suspicious. Millie talked all the time. My other job was to avoid speaking to the blond-haired, droopy-eyed boy in tights and lavender *knickers* now approaching with his father. The two commands completely contradicted each other.

"Earl William. You remember my niece, Millie."

The Earl bowed. "Yes, of course, Your Highness. I do believe she attended school with my son."

"Hey, Millie," Gavin said, bored.

"Hello, Gavin," I said back in the same tone. Two

70

words. Millie wouldn't give me a bad PPR for two words, would she?

Auntie Ostrich glared at me. "Millie was just telling me how much she loved your gift."

Earl William I could talk to. I positioned my body so it was clear who was being addressed. "Yes, it's a lovely vase." I paused, flashing again to Millie's profile. Talk fast and a lot. "We have it in our main sitting area. It catches the light perfectly and makes a pretty double rainbow on the wall. I love rainbows, don't you? I use to have this wild dress when I was little that had all these colors—"

"Now, child," Auntie Ostrich chided, "let's not bore the earl with unnecessary details."

The earl chuckled. "I have heard of your . . . how do they say it . . . gift for gab, Your Highness. And now that I know how much you appreciate our country's fine crystal, I'll make sure to take note for future gifts."

"Oh, you are too kind, Earl William," Auntie Ostrich said. "Now, let's leave these schoolmates to their youthful conversation. I'm sure they have much to talk about, and I must show you my recently purchased paintings."

Earl William escorted Auntie away. Gavin rubbed his nose and yawned.

Ahhh!! The warning bell rang over and over in my head. Yes, I'd managed to become chatterbox Millie and still avoided talking to Gavin, but now it was just the two of us. I so wanted to do this right, and Millie had been clear in her profile. Don't say anything. Don't say anything. Don't say—

"So someone said you were taking fall off to travel the world or some such," Gavin asked.

I did a halfhearted shrug.

Gavin scratched his chin. "I get so tired of traveling sometimes. Museums can be so tedious. Same with monasteries and castles and vineyards. And yes, I *know* my family owns a large Renoir collection, but do I need to *see* it? You've seen one famous old painting, you've seen them all. Right?"

I readjusted my wig. Genevieve said if I tuned in to my magic, it would be strengthened. Was there an internal switch inside me that made it go on? Or did I first have to figure out the special emotion she was talking about? If mine was boredom, then magic would have been swirling out of my ears right then. This guy went on and on and on and. . . .

"Now, I did travel to Greece this summer. Excellent cuisine there in Greece. Doesn't quite compare to some of the costal towns in Italy, but what does? I had this prosciutto in Sicily once that was divine. Perfect amount of marbling in the fat. . . ."

Good gravy. Now would be a fabulous time for that magic to kick in. Any minute. Just zap this kid away. And . . . go. ZAP.

No wonder Millie was so annoyed that Gavin thought she liked him. If I could talk, I would yell at him to stop telling such pompous snories. Sorry, stories.

". . . and then I said, I don't care if you're the Duke of the Whole World, I still want a rematch!" He burst into laughter and slapped his knee.

I smiled weakly at his lame joke, scanning the crowd

for a getaway. Technically, I was still in the clear. I wasn't speaking. But at some point he was going to expect a sound from me. I had to escape.

"You know, I always thought you were a tad chatty for my tastes. But you're actually quite agreeable. Lynette told me you fancy me. Maybe if we spent more time together, something could . . . blossom."

I tensed. Talk about backfire. All this guy wanted was someone quiet so he could listen to himself talk. But being quiet was my instruction. What was I supposed to do? "Er . . ."

He stared at me expectedly, like of course Millie was going to jump at a chance with him. I'd rather jump off a bridge.

This was not something BEST prepared me for. But as much as I hated to admit it, someone *had* groomed me for this situation during Level One training. Lilith.

Wait, this WAS the situation I'd practiced with Lilith! Art museum with a great-aunt. Had she known then that I would be here now? No, of course she couldn't have. Besides, the strategies she'd taught me would work at any time. Like now.

Show him my jewelry? No, he wouldn't care.

Change the subject? He would be more encouraged to ramble.

Laryngitis! That's it.

My resolve wavered. All during Level One training I'd been so set on impacting these princesses. As Meredith suggested, I had used my MP to guide my choices, even when the choices had been out of character for the princess. Now I was doing exactly as Lilith instructed—I personified Millie. Full Method. I had to get Millie out of this situation *without* breaking character.

I grabbed my throat and made my voice sound hoarse. "Sore."

Gavin stepped back. "Oh, don't get me ill. I have to speak at an orphanage tomorrow because my family is an important donor. We donated *quite a bit* of money to those urchins. Quite a bit. Not too much, naturally, but enough to warrant recognition. Orphanages are rather passé, though, so when I'm in charge of the family holdings I'd like to concentrate instead on—"

I pointed to my throat. "Water." I rushed across the room to the bar, and asked for a glass of water. Why did it always seem like I was running away on this job? Gavin blinked at me, surprised that someone he thought was so enamored with him would leave so quickly. I raised my glass to him as if to say, *See? Can't talk. Gotta drink.*

The orchestra broke into a waltz. Couples filled the dance floor. I almost choked when Gavin began to make his way over to me. Sweat trickled down my back, which might've had something to do with the corset. I took another sip of water and steadied myself against a table before barreling ahead to the bathroom. I was almost there when a girl around my age with a yellow dress and hair curled like Goldilocks attacked me with a hug.

"Millie! Where have you been? I love, love, love your

costume. Isn't mine the best? I want to bring corsets back into fashion and I'm also thinking these wigs are . . . Hey, did I see you talking to Gavin? Is it true that you like him?"

I shook my head and pointed at my throat, glad my idea could carry over to another conversation. "Can't talk. Laryngitis."

"Then don't talk. Listen. Did you hear who is coming tonight? Princess Elsa. She's from that country that ceased to exist after . . . oh, I can't remember what war. She's still royalty, though. Her grandmother has insulted every royal in this room, and then some. Have you heard of her?"

"Hmmm . . ." I squinted at the ceiling like I was trying to place her name, when really my insides were doing the cha-cha. Elsa? Here? I might meet a former client? How surreal would that be? Even more, what if she was here with Karl?

Seriously, WHAT IF SHE WAS HERE WITH KARL?

"She's right over there." The girl gave a discreet nod, and there was Elsa, dressed in a steel gray Empire-waisted gown, her blond hair wrapped in a loose bun. Disappointment punched me when I realized she was alone. No, it was good. No need to complicate the love triangle.

Okay, Karl had no idea I existed, so it was more like a love line.

"I can't believe she came," said the girl. "She's pretty enough, but I doubt I'd join the scene if I had her grandmother's reputation to live down. I can't decide if she's brave or stupid."

"She's not stupid," I said.

"Wait, I thought you said your throat hurt." Goldilocks scowled. "And how do you know her?"

I coughed, making my voice scratchy. "She could be nice. I don't know."

Out of the corner of my eye, I saw Gavin approaching. Goldilocks was still blocking the door to the bathroom. I had nowhere to go. He bowed. "Ladies."

Goldilocks giggled. I swallowed.

"Millie, may I grant upon you the the honor of dancing with me?"

Grrrrrrreat. I tapped on my throat.

He shook his head.

"The orphans will have to live with it if I get sick. Tonight, we dance!"

Chapter
8

*G*avin took my hand and led me to the floor. Like most everything in the time right before the French Revolution, the minuet is pure fluff. Lots of slow turns and twirls and bows and tiptoeing around. The styles then were not particularly masculine, and so it was far from attractive to see Gavin in his ghastly knickers (with bows, BOWS), his chest puffed out as he pranced around the floor.

I did my best to concentrate on the steps I'd practiced over the summer. I was doing well enough until Elsa joined midway through. It was hard not to look at the girl I had pretended to be; but really, everyone in the room was watching her anyway. She moved through the steps with ease, like she'd always been in royal circles and not milking goats just last summer.

We made eye contact once, when she caught me staring. Elsa narrowed her eyes like she was trying to place my face. The scrutiny shouldn't have worried me—she wasn't seeing *my* face, after all. But we were still linked in a weird way. Maybe that's what she sensed.

The costume didn't help matters much. I might have looked like Millie on the outside, but my insides were still Desi. The hearty meal I'd indulged in with Genevieve did not go well with the tight dress. And Gavin was sweating. And he smelled like a hunting hound trapped in nylon. And did I mention the knicker bows?

The music, thankfully, ended, and I turned to escape.

"Another?" Gavin asked, his eyes bright.

I tried to pull away from his firm grip. "Need to find my aunt."

"But when will we have the opportunity to dance again?"

"Hopefully never."

"What's that?"

"Oh, um, it could be forever!"

The next dance started, this time a bourrée, which was much more lively and quick. The splendor and sounds whirled around me. I felt like I was Donna Reed in *It's a Wonderful Life*, except in Technicolor. Really bright Technicolor. Like, I-want-to-throw-up-now-the-lights-are-all-flashing *Technicolor*.

The colors blurred into blackness. Not good. Not good AT ALL. I searched wildly and made eye contact with Elsa again. She broke away from her partner, rushed over, and hugged me. No, *pretended* to hug me. She was actually holding me up.

"I'm sorry to interrupt your dance, but hi! I'm so happy to see you!"

I was too busy inhaling air to ask how the heck Elsa knew Millie. Not only was this Elsa's first royal event, but Goldilocks had made it clear that these two ran in very different circles.

"Um, you too?"

"Can I steal her away?" she asked Gavin. "It's been so long, and I want to make sure we get a moment before the night ends."

Gavin didn't answer at first, probably because he was too busy staring at Elsa in complete awe. "Of . . . of course. And I don't believe *we've* been introduced. I would remember if we had." He bowed. "I'm Lord Gavin."

Elsa gave a royal nod. "A pleasure, my lord. I am Princess Elsa of Holdenzastein."

"The pleasure is mine, Your Highness. *All mine.*" Gavin chortled.

I choked back a laugh. What I wouldn't give to tell Kylee about this clown.

"Now, please pardon us." Elsa squeezed my elbow. "I'll return her later."

We wove back into the museum lobby and found a bench. The stars winked through the triangular windowpanes of the pyramid.

"I hope that wasn't presumptuous of me, but you looked like you needed some help in there. Here, I'll get you some water." Elsa left, returning with a tall glass. She waited until I was done gulping before she spoke. "I'm Elsa."

So they didn't know each other. I dabbed at my forehead with Millie's lacy handkerchief. "Millie. Well, Princess Millie."

Elsa's face reddened. "I'm sorry. I'm not used to titles. I'm close enough to the royals I know that we don't use them."

Close to the royals. Close to Prince Karl. The words sliced through me. I painted on a smile. "You saved me. You can call me whatever you want."

"Do you feel all right now?"

"Yes. Corsets."

"Silliest invention ever. I cheated and went into the early nineteenth century with my costume."

"Your dress is gorgeous, by the way."

She fingered the fabric. "Thanks. My nana made it, actually. But if anyone else asks me the designer, I'll make up someone that sounds really French."

I laughed. I liked her. She was how she seemed in her journal—down-to-earth. Funnier than I would have thought, and more assertive.

"So who are the royals in your social circle? Any . . . cute boys?" I asked. I knew what her answer would be. I knew it would hurt to hear it. But I still had to ask.

"Oh, just family." Elsa's voice was guarded. "This is one of my first events."

Was the cute-boy question too personal? I wanted Elsa to feel comfortable around me. Around Millie. Despite the two-year age difference, I could see them being friends. So I did what Millie did best: I chattered. "I'm traveling with my aunt this season. She's big on keeping her schedule packed. It's been fun, but these events can get old. Always having to be ON, you know? And some of the people are . . . well, you met Gavin."

"I'm sure he's a nice enough boy, but . . ." Elsa shuddered. "Those bows on his pants were horrific."

"I had drama with him in the past. This girl at school told him that I liked him, so he went and blabbed that around and acted way better than me and . . . Sorry." Wow, I was getting good at this rambling thing. "It's a long story."

"Don't worry about it. It's nice to sit back and listen for a while. I'm on display tonight, what with this being a debut for me. I almost feel like it's not real, you know? Like I'm only pretending to be someone else. Do you ever feel like that?"

It's in my job description. "I think that's part of being royal. Putting on airs. Which is why I'm so grateful that you saved me from having to pretend to care what Gavin was saying."

"You can pay me back someday." Elsa jumped up from the bench. "Now, speaking of putting on airs, I need to go talk to another of my nana's enemies and try to repair old wounds. I hope we meet again, Princess Millie."

Elsa melted back into the throngs, smiling and chatting like she'd worked similar rooms million of times. I found Auntie Ostrich and stayed with her for the final hours of the party, gabbing to her friends about Millie's frivolous life details (string beans are *way* better than peas!). The corset and constant conversation exhausted me, enough that I nearly cried tears of relief when my Rouge timer went off while Auntie Ostrich and I were in the hotel elevator, on the way up to our suite.

"What's that sound?" she asked.

The timer hardly made a noise. It just vibrated. Sheesh, aren't old people supposed to have hearing problems?

"Nothing." I clutched my purse tightly. "Must be my dress rustling."

The elevator door opened. Auntie's bodyguard took her hand and helped her out. I ran over to the door of our penthouse suite, the only door on the floor.

"Be patient," she scolded me as the bodyguard slid the key into the lock. "Your anxiousness is hardly ladylike."

I could feel the corset loosening, which also meant the rouge was wearing off. My clock had struck midnight, and I had to get away from Auntie Ostrich before she saw me turn into a pumpkin.

"I have to . . . I have to use the little princess room," I said.

Auntie Ostrich wrinkled her nose in disgust. "Gracious! Then hurry. Go change and wash up as well. And when you return, we must have a talk about your vulgarity."

I'm sure Millie wasn't going to like her welcome-home lecture, but what could I do? I turned to my room.

"Millie?" Auntie Ostrich paused. "Are you feeling well? You seem . . . well, you seem *taller*."

"I'm fine," I replied, but Millie's voice sounded too much like my own. I yanked open the door and locked it behind me. "Just had a long evening." I called.

The bubble was already waiting in Millie's room. Auntie Ostrich pounded on the door. "Now you have me concerned. Did something make you ill?"

I garbled a reply before sticking one leg into the bubble. The last thing I saw was another bubble nearby and the real Millie stepping out. She froze when she saw me. Who knows what she saw—half Desi, half her. I mouthed, "Pretend you're sick," before I disappeared into Meredith's office.

I better not have blown my cover in those last few moments. Sub Spottings are HUGE deals at Façade. I looked to Meredith, who sat at her desk, fuming.

"Sit down," she ordered.

I sighed. Unlike Cinderella, it seemed I hadn't made it out in time.

Chapter
9

Meredith pounded her hand on the desk. "What do you have to say for yourself?"

"I couldn't get away! We're lucky I didn't start to transform in the elevator. Couldn't you guys give me more notice? Millie told me not to get caught by her aunt, and now I'm sure—"

"No one cares about *that*."

"I care! I was doing great before the Rouge wore off, and that's saying a lot considering how stupid the whole thing was. Dumb paintings and corsets and silly dancing and—"

"I'm not talking about your *gig*. You didn't have a large overlap. You weren't Sub Spotted."

"I'm not going to get sub sanitized then?" I shuddered at the idea. Sub sanitizing involved having a sub's entire experience washed from memory.

"Don't be ridiculous. Sometimes the Rouge schedule is off—that's not your fault."

I slumped into the chair opposite Meredith. The way we transitioned in and out of these jobs was risky. It would have been awful to make it through all the rest of the night's craziness, only to change back into Desi and blow Millie's cover. "Then why are you . . . interrogating me?"

"I'd like you to explain this." Meredith held out a silver business card. Printed in red ink on very thick paper were the words, *Please call Genevieve*.

I took the card and flipped to the back. There was a symbol of an Egyptian beetle and nothing else. "No contact information. Haven't you guys thought of cell phones?"

"That calling cards gives you *permission* to call upon her if you need to. With this card, all you have to do is say her name out loud and she'll contact you. She didn't give *me* one until I was an agent. So I'd like to know what went down at Dorshire Hall that would make her bestow one on a spanking-new Level Two."

"Noth . . . nothing. We talked about magic. The history . . . general stuff."

"Well, it couldn't have been *too* general. She's taken an interest in you. She wants you to report back if you have any magical occurrences. Did you have anything magical happen on this last job?"

85

"No." Dancing with Gavin was anything but magical. "I tried, actually, but nothing came. I used common sense and Millie's princess profile. Same stuff I did as a Level One, except everything went more by the book."

"Humph." Meredith sat down on the couch and rubbed her temples. "So we're clear here, you didn't say anything about *me* to Genevieve. Anything that could hurt my chances at this promotion. Anything . . . personal."

I widened my eyes. The anger and suspicion all made sense now. She thought I'd snitched about her prince. "Meredith. Of course not. I would never say anything bad about you. We did talk about your hair. And Genevieve said you were a hardworking sub."

"Good." Meredith shot me another murderous look. "Because if you ever did—"

"I'm not Lilith."

Meredith blew out a breath. "You're right. You're not." She paused. "Well, you have that card. Be careful with it. This agency . . . You don't have to tell them everything. You never know how the information, or even your talents, might be used. So think before you speak. Understood?"

"But I have nothing to hide."

"Of course *you* don't." Meredith pushed her chair back. "Well! You should probably change before you get back to your play auditions. Your clothes and gift basket are by the couch. Take out what you need, and I'll drop the rest off in your bedroom on my way out of town."

"All right," I said slowly. The only thing that scared me

more than Meredith being feisty was Meredith faking nice. After she closed her office door, I changed back into my jeans, ditching the Shakespeare T-shirt for one of my new tops—robin's egg blue with ruffles down the neckline. Most important, it was a lightweight fabric that would save me from further sweating disasters.

Because of the Law of Duplicity, I'd only left the high school theater bathroom a second before, so it was still empty when I exited the bubble. It always took me a moment to realize where I was, what time it was. *Who* I was. Desi. Back to Desi, who was still in the middle of auditions.

Auditions. Stress! Still . . . better than a Gavin chat. Kissing Lilith's feet would be better than a Gavin chat.

I splashed cold water on my face, patted it dry with a scratchy paper towel, and thought of the luxurious hand towels waiting for me in my basket. And the calling card in my back pocket. I pulled it out and rubbed my fingers over the embossed lettering. Would I ever use it? What would happen when I called Genevieve? Did she only want to know if I felt magic at work, or at home too? And why did Genevieve give it to *me* of all people?

The bathroom door swung open, and I shoved the card into my back pocket.

Kylee grinned when she saw me. "What's taking you so long?"

Just had to use the bathroom. Oh, and hop over to Paris.

Exciting things are always *more* exciting when you can talk about them, not lock them away. I swallowed back the urge to tell Kylee everything. "Um . . . just easing my nerves."

"I saw Reed!" Kylee said. "He did such an amazing job. He's like . . . who's that New Zealand actor? The tall one? That's going to bug me. Anyway, I sat two rows back from him and almost got up the nerve to say hi, which I'm going to count as a win. . . . Hey. Where did you get that shirt?"

Whoops. I was so glad to be free of the sweat trap, I didn't even think about a costume change explanation, especially to someone as observant as Kylee. I tugged on the hem.

"I brought an extra. My SHAKESPEARE ROCKETH shirt was so tight, it got all sweaty. Besides"—my laugh rang out high and false—"it's the theater! Costume changes are part of the deal."

"I've never seen you wear it before."

"It's new."

"It's cute. Where did you get it?"

"My mom bought it for me."

Kylee came closer and checked the back tag. "Desi, it's by Floressa Chase. That shirt had to cost over a hundred dollars."

"Really?" I fingered the fabric. "My mom probably got it on sale."

Kylee shook her head. "Anyway, they're about to call people to do to partner readings. You ready?"

I pushed my hair away from my face and smoothed out

my shirt. It's amazing what a quick stint as a princess can do for your acting confidence.

"Yeah. Let's go."

Kylee and I linked arms and walked into the theater.

I stayed up that night, worrying about Genevieve's calling card, picturing the look on Meredith's face when she said to be careful. Be careful of what?

And I had other questions to consider. Was I in trouble? Did Genevieve trust me? Was Façade reconsidering my advancement? They had to be pleased with my performance. Aside from the messy bubble exit, I'd done everything Millie asked. And my other clients were happy—I saw firsthand how well I'd positively impacted Elsa's life. And the customer is always right. Right?

It was past midnight when I finally fell asleep.

By four the next afternoon, I'd swigged three Mountain Dews to give me the energy to face the cast list being posted any minute in the high school cafeteria. I took a seat away from the cliques and stared at the mural of the school mascot, the Spud (which was a large potato. Yes, the other teams always threatened to mash us. At least we weren't the Boise Beets). After five minutes of examining the Spudster, I got out the new BEST list Meredith had sent that morning.

The tasks read more like a celebrity-assistant checklist than a mastery of royal skills. I could check through them in weeks, rather than the months it initially took me to prepare for Millie:

89

1. Acting
2. Celebrity gossip
3. Familiarity with the fashion industry, including relevant designers and their point of view
4. Fashion design and basic sewing skills
5. Yachting

This princess was going to be awesome, but the list still had its challenges. Yachting? How do you practice yachting in Sproutville? And I designed my own T-shirts, but I didn't follow the latest trends. Plus, I could hardly sew on a button.

My gaze returned to the Spud as I strategized ways I could fit BEST into my schoolwork. My view was soon blocked, however, by Celeste and Hayden. I gave them a polite, *why-are-you-standing-here* smile.

Hayden pulled out a seat and sat at my table. "Hey, Daisy."

"You don't need to sit by her." Celeste rolled her eyes. "We're already on the edge of dorkdom as eighth graders here, no need to go completely geek."

"Sorry, babe." Hayden stood. "Can we hurry, though? I have practice at five."

"I said I have to ask her something."

"Hi," I finally said. "I'm guessing I'm 'her,' right? So I'm sitting right here in case you want to have a conversation *with* me instead of *about* me."

"Oh." Celeste flipped her hair. "Your mom was supposed

to give me a ride home, but I'm going to Hayden's practice instead. But tell her we're still on for my fitting next week. And we have to turn in our head shots for the pageant Web site."

"Sure. I love being your messenger girl."

Either my sarcasm was lost on Celeste or she chose to ignore it, because I went right back to being invisible. "Now that *that's* over with, I need some candy."

Hayden nuzzled her neck. "I can give you some sugar."

It took every ounce of self-control not to gag. Luckily, a girl walked into the cafeteria with a piece of white paper in hand, which she stuck on the announcement board. Celeste forgot my invisibility and looked at me, wide-eyed. "Do you think that's—"

I shot out of my chair. "The cast list."

We rushed over to the glowing white paper. Celeste pushed her way through the crowd. "Peaseblossom! A fairy! I'm one of the main fairies! OMG, I'm going to look so fabulous."

Hayden snatched her to the side and proceeded to give her a victory kiss. Great. There were probably two parts actually going to eighth graders, and of course Celeste got one of them. Now she would have to squeeze rehearsals in between all her time bonding with my mother and practicing her pageant wave. I shrank back from the crowd, waiting for a turn.

Someone tapped my shoulder and whispered, "Did you see your name yet?"

I glanced back at Reed, who wore a confident smile and a vintage plaid shirt. "I'm too nervous."

"Do you need some muscle?"

"I'll wait."

"Oh, come on. You're dying to know. So am I." Reed tugged on my arm and led me through the mob. I bit a hangnail as he scanned down the female sheet.

"That's too bad."

"I'm not on there, am I? Now I'm going to have to listen to Celeste go on about her fairy-ness—"

"Oh, no. You're on there. It's too bad for that Celeste girl. She's going to have some serious jealousy issues."

"Really? Why?"

"Look at the top." Reed gave my arm a playful squeeze. "You're Titania. The Queen of the Fairies."

My stomach dropped down into my intestines, where it proceeded to do a dance and twist itself around all my other organs until my entire body was one inner-dancing bounty of glee. I breathed deeply, trying to control the frenzy of emotions that were overtaking me. It wasn't like the buzzing I'd felt during auditions. No, this was a Moment. A real-life, nothing to do with subbing or Celeste or anyone but me *Moment*.

I got one of the girl leads. As an eighth grader.

Seriously, aside from the whole job-as-a-substitute-princess thing, this was the biggest news in my life. Weren't fairies usually petite like Celeste? I hope the boys weren't short. Boys. I hadn't even scanned those yet. Celeste was already in front of the list.

"I'll talk to someone." She turned to Hayden and made a pouty face. "You have to get a part! I'll be so lonely without you."

Hayden could barely keep from smiling with relief. "I know, it's a bummer, but I have soccer and stuff."

She wrapped her arms around his waist. I caught a bit of their conversation as they walked toward the cafeteria doors. "I just want to be with you all the time."

"Me too, babe. But you're going to be hot as a fairy."

"I know, right?"

They were so perfect for each other. It was almost embarrassing to think I had ever had a crush on that guy. Or been friends with Celeste. I felt like an entirely different person now. One who was STARRING IN A PLAY!

I stood there, in that cafeteria, until the crowd left and the noise quieted. When only a few stragglers remained, I got the courage to look at the cast list again. It was still there. *Desi Bascomb. Titania, Fairy Queen.*

I touched my name on the white paper.

Reed leaned against the wall, a smile playing on his lips. "Making sure it's real?"

"You do you see my name up there, right? It's not my wish turning into some alternative reality."

"You're a queen. Almost as good as an ass."

"Sorry?"

"The ass. Donkey. Nick Bottom. The comic relief of the play."

"You're Bottom?"

"Yes. He's the one who wanders into the forest and gets a donkey head halfway through, but you still like me, which is sweet. Kind of hurts that it's all because of the love potion, but you're married, so it's probably for the best."

"I know what happens in *Midsummer*. It's just . . . you're . . . you're *Bottom*?"

"Hee-haw." He tapped the sheet of paper, right by his name. "Gotta get going. See you at rehearsal."

What Reed didn't say was that Titania and Bottom had a kissing scene. And true, in a play with mixed identities and affections, there is bound to be kissing. But I hadn't even considered the possibility of Reed and me kissing. Again and again. It wasn't anything like the dunk tank incident—this was conscious, live, in-front-of-everyone (including my best friend) *kissing*.

Shakespeare was suddenly a lot more interesting.

Chapter
10

I didn't tell Kylee about the kissing part. She would read way too much into it, just like when Reed gave me CPR. I knew a stage kiss meant nothing. Besides, I was going to hook them up, and once that happened, any Shakespearean lip-business wasn't going to matter.

The hookup was going to take some effort, though, because Kylee got stage fright—make that *Reed* fright—at the thought of talking to him. We waited in the back row of the theater on the first day of rehearsal so Kylee could accidentally on purpose run into him. She paced the aisle, her expression determined, like when she was playing a difficult piece on her clarinet.

"So we'll see him," Kylee said. "You'll say hi and remind him who I am. Then I'll say . . ."

"Hi," I said. "Or hello. You can improvise that part."

"Don't make fun of me! I like to have everything planned out when I'm nervous."

"You talked to him the very first time we met," I said.

"And then we didn't see him all summer, which has given me plenty of time to build up our next encounter." Kylee stopped pacing and bit at a nail.

"The word *encounter* makes me think of alien abductions."

"Aha!" She pumped her fist in the air. "You've ditched the old movies and entered my world of scary. Next up, swamp creatures."

"No. Never. And Kylee, be like this around him. You're funny."

Kylee and I jumped when the doors opened. Two junior girls brushed past us. Kylee fanned herself. "Is it possible to have a stroke when you're thirteen?"

The doors opened again, and this time it *was* Reed. I pinched the back of Kylee's arm and whispered, "Talk."

"Hey, girls." He swung an arm around our shoulders like we were all old friends, like Kylee wasn't about to pass out.

"Hey," I said.

"Hi, er . . . hello," Kylee said.

"You ready for the most boring day of your life?" Reed asked.

I looked up at Reed, which I appreciated. There weren't

that many guys tall enough for me to actually look up to. "Why do you say that?"

"First day is full read-through." Reed dropped his arms and hooked his fingers under the straps of his backpack. "Sometimes they're fun, but with it being Shakespeare, it'll be auditory sleeping pills."

Kylee snorted, then covered her nose.

"You know that other eighth grader, Celeste?" I asked. "Well, my mom is her pageant coach, and I've sat through some of their training sessions. Nothing more boring than that."

Kylee nodded, but again, *said nothing*.

"Come!" Mrs. Olman was standing center stage, her arms outstretched. "Actors! Let us convene!"

Reed grimaced. "Longest day ever. I promise."

"Well, we better get up there." I nudged Kylee again. "Have fun teaching band, Kylee. Did I mention Kylee helps teach high school band? She's super talented."

"I think you did mention that. Sounds cool."

"Yeah. So . . . um . . . see you guys." Kylee paused. "Stay awake."

Reed laughed. "Later, Kylee."

Kylee stepped back like his farewell had hit her with physical force. When Reed ran up the steps of the stage, I turned to Kylee. "The stay-awake line was funny. But you need to talk more."

She shook her head. "I don't know if I can. He's, like, a good-looking guy Medusa: I just freeze up when I see him."

Mrs. Olman clapped her hands. "Actors!"

"Thanks for helping." Kylee trudged out of the theater.

Well, I tried. I couldn't stick Royal Rouge on and talk for the girl. I lumbered onto the stage and took a seat next to Reed. I thought I was ready for the rehearsal—I'd steered clear of the Mountain Dew, and I was wearing a tank top to avoid sweat problems—but nothing could have prepared me for an hour and a half straight of Shakespeare's English. It didn't matter that this was the shortened version of the play—half the cast fell asleep, and it became an unspoken rule that we would elbow one another before our parts. Mrs. Olman kept reminding us to enunciate the words and feel, FEEL! the character's soul, but even she left to get some coffee during the fourth act.

Reed and I had two scenes together—in the first, Titania falls in love with Bottom, thanks to a love potion. As Mrs. Olman said, the more I acted in love, the funnier the scene would be.

"What angel wakes me from my flowery bed?"

Reed scooted to the edge of his seat. He cleared his throat and delivered his line. Perfectly. Like everything he did.

"Uh . . ." I scrolled through the words and delivered my next line.

He leaned in, and I could smell his cologne—sporty mixed with something else. The ocean? "You might want to project a bit more," he whispered.

I said my next line loud and clear. Very loud and clear.

"You don't need to project *that* much," Reed said.

"Thanks." I clasped my hands in my lap, resisting the urge to swat him.

"Let's take a break," suggested Mrs. Olman. The cast members broke into chattering groups. Reed bumped me with his elbow.

"You're nervous."

"I'm fine."

"Do you want some advice?"

"If I do, I'll ask the director."

"It helps if you can find the truth of the character. Like, Titania may be acting one way, but feeling something else. If you can recognize the difference in what the character *wants* to say and what she is *actually* saying, you can add a lot of depth to the role."

Depth? He wanted *depth*? Hello, I wasn't even fourteen yet and I'd already worked two jobs (one of them magical), run a small Internet business, made good grades, and got a part in this play. Not to mention I was a pretty nice person and didn't obsess over shallow, non-obsess-worthy things, like what cologne Reed was wearing and why it smelled so nice. I was the Grand Canyon of depth!

"Thanks. I'll think about that."

After the break, Mrs. Olman offered a few tips on speaking slowly to convey the meaning of the words. Reed nudged me like I should pull out a pencil and write everything down because she was obviously talking to me.

As annoying as his "pointers" were, I was motivated to improve my delivery. If I could channel the same feelings I'd had during tryouts, not even Shakespeare's stupid old language could stop me from shining. I just had to figure out *how* I'd tapped in to those feelings.

I closed my eyes for a second. *Okay, I'm Titania. My husband has been a total jerk to me. Plus, I'm under a love spell. What would that be like, to feel a strong emotion that's not authentic?*

A familiar spark grew inside of me. I squirmed in recognition. I had felt the princesses' emotions, but they were still secondhand. A love potion would do the same thing—take away the honesty of emotion. I understood Titania—she believed in a feeling that wasn't real. The spark grew until I almost burst. I was so Titania in that moment, I could have sprouted fairy wings and flown across the theater.

When I said my lines, Reed's mouth went slack.

"What?" I whispered.

He shook his head. "Wow."

Wow was right. It took another scene before I stopped shaking. It reminded me of this time when I was seven, when my family was in an accident that totaled my mom's car. Everyone was fine, but I remember sitting on the curb, nearly in shock and dizzy from the adrenaline. This feeling wasn't as intense, but the buzzing topped any sugar or caffeine rush I'd ever had.

I was back to regular Desi by the end of the read-through, which Reed was right about—take away the

Titania moments, and the last two hours made my Top Ten Most Tiring Moments of My Life list, right after my dance with Gavin. We slumped out of the theater looking defeated, Mrs. Olman especially. It was hard to imagine how those words—words half of us couldn't even pronounce well, let alone understand—were going to transform into something watchable or entertaining.

Once I was outside, though, I stopped to smile at the warmth of the sun. So it wasn't my favorite play ever. So what. I'd gotten a big part in a HIGH SCHOOL PLAY. That play could have been *Fluffy the Bunny Hops to Happyland* and I would have been stoked.

I wandered over to the football-field entrance, where I'd told my mom to pick me up. Almost everyone else had cars or friends with cars, and I didn't want to be the loser eighth grader waiting for mommy directly in front of the school. I dropped my backpack and gulped some water from the drinking fountain. Reed was standing next to me when I came up. "Did you do what I told you to?" he asked.

I grabbed my chest. "Ahhh! You scared me. What's with everyone popping up on me like that?"

"What do you mean?"

"Nothing." I took a few deep breaths.

"So when you read those lines . . . what did you do differently?"

"Oh. Um . . ." I still didn't know *what* I had done. Genevieve said it wasn't possible for me to use my magic in my real life, yet I knew something had happened. I could tell by how I felt, by other's reactions. I doubted the other actors thought they were about to get "fairified." It wasn't normal. Maybe it was a touch of magic, not enough for the agency to be aware of it, but enough to give me a push. Or maybe it was more, and I needed to tell Genevieve? I'd have to think about that. "I don't know. What you said. I tried to feel what the character felt."

"Did you do that when you auditioned?" he asked.

I shrugged. "Pretty much. Why, did I suck?"

"No. You . . . you're . . . really talented, Desi."

I blushed at the unexpected compliment. "Well, that was just a few lines. You were on all day."

"I've had a lot of practice. But you . . . you should do whatever you just did again. Every time."

"Um, all right."

Reed stared at me a couple more seconds. I was starting to wonder if staring at people so long was some New Zealand thing that didn't translate into our culture.

"So, I'm going to go." I backed away from his unflinching gaze. "Uh . . . bye."

Reed stepped forward, and I caught another whiff of his cologne. Wow, where did he buy that stuff? "Wait. Sorry, I'm acting weird, aren't I?"

I didn't answer.

"I do that sometimes. Sorry." He fiddled with his backpack strap. "I'm trying to figure you out. Because, you know, we'll be acting together, so it helps if you have a sort of understanding of your scene mate."

"Staring someone down doesn't get you understood. It gets you slapped."

Reed cracked a smile. "You've got to be the funniest American I've met."

"On behalf of my country, thank you."

"Here, I'll tell you what." He tapped my leg with his foot. "Let me prove to you I'm not crazy. I'll give you a ride home."

"You have a car?" I asked. It wasn't unheard of for ninth graders to drive—the Idaho driving age was fifteen.

"Ah, not yet. But I do have Lola." He pointed at the sole bike on the bike rack. A tandem bike.

"You ride a two-person bicycle by yourself?"

"Got her at a garage sale this summer." Reed walked over and kicked a tire. "The couple that bought her broke up, and it hurt the poor guy to look at it. I swindled it for thirty bucks. Decent workout, but it's definitely better if you have another rider. Increases velocity. So are you in?"

"My mom is supposed to pick me up."

"Call her."

I chewed on my lip. I'd never ridden a two-person bike; it looked like fun. If only I could swap places with Kylee right now and let her bike with Reed. But she was still in the band room, so the next best thing was to hang out with Reed *for* her, right?

"Okay." I texted my mom. Even if she missed the text, chances were she'd notice a tandem bike on the road. "Anything I should know?"

"I'm the captain, you're the stoker. Which basically means I steer, brake, and yell if we hit a wall. You have the difficult job of taking in the scenery."

"Let's not harm any walls on this journey, okay?"

Reed gave me his helmet, and I swung my leg over the side of the bike. He eased onto the front seat and tooted his horn. "You ready?"

Again, a whole conversation without mentioning Kylee. I was a lousy friend. "One more thing. You know how you said I was the funniest girl you've ever met?"

"Funniest American."

"Sure. Wait until you get to know Kylee. She's hilarious."

Reed turned around and gave me a weird look. "That was the most random thing you've ever said."

"Just pedal."

Reed steered us out of the parking lot and onto a back road. His calm control made up for my wobbliness. He called out whenever he made a turn or saw a bump. I pointed out Sproutville landmarks. Or, rather, made up landmarks.

"See that house?" I pointed to a white brick rambler.

"Yeah?"

"Mark Twain used to live there."

"Huh? The guy who wrote *Tom Sawyer*?"

"Close. Actually, it's an auto tech named Mark Wayne."

Reed laughed. I liked his laugh. And despite his weird staring problem, Reed was easy to talk to. I didn't get why Kylee froze up around him.

Mom was pulling out of the driveway when we biked up. She unrolled her window and stuck her head out. "When you texted that you were riding a two-person bike, I thought it was a joke."

"No, Mom. Tandem biking is very serious." I hopped off the bike and handed Reed his helmet. When he stuck it on, a strand of hair got in his eye. I almost brushed it away, just to be nice, but stopped myself because . . . because I don't know why.

"Do I get an introduction?" Mom asked. "Aren't you the nice boy who saved Desi from that dunk tank?"

"Yep, that's me. Dunk Tank Superhero. Saving the world one drowned girl at a time."

"Oh, you're a charmer." Mom giggled. "Isn't he *charming*, Desi?"

I rolled my eyes. "Bye, Reed."

"Thanks for the pedal power." He honked his horn and biked away.

"You didn't tell me *Reed* is in the play."

"There are a lot of boys in the play." I started to walk toward the house. "It's Shakespeare—there used to be ONLY boys in his plays."

"That's fine. But I'm here if you want to talk about it more." Mom closed the door behind us and hung her keys on the hook.

I crossed my arms. "And Reed is Kylee's crush, if that's what you're getting at."

"I'm not getting at anything." Mom tried to hide a smug

smile, but I saw it. Saw it and hated it. There was nothing to be smug about.

I ran up to my room and dropped onto my bed. I needed to call Kylee, but first I needed to take a nap. The bike ride and the using-magic-to-be-like-Titania thing had drained me.

I sat up. Magic. There it was again. If that was really what I'd experienced, then Genevieve would want to know. I flopped down and closed my eyes. Now I just had to find the courage to use the card.

That night, I did my homework for the week, skimmed two yachting catalogues, and clicked through eight celebrity gossip sites (research rocks!) before I took the calling card out of my desk drawer. I placed it on my pillow and lay down next to it, staring at the pictures on my Wall o' Awesome Things. They were mostly pictures of my favorite old celebrities. And Karl. Over the last couple of months, I'd added quite a few pictures of Karl.

I hated to admit it, but part of my motivation for wanting to do well with Façade was the prospect of seeing Karl again. Royal circles were small. Whether I subbed for Elsa or Karl's girlfriend, Duchess Olivia, or some random royal at a charity event, our paths were bound to cross. I didn't know what I would do or say. If I had magic, like really real magic that I could channel and use to my bidding, it would be mighty tempting to somehow get him to kiss me again. Kiss me, then date me in a few years, marry me in a few more, have some royal sons that would make nice princes and . . .

I kicked at my wall. I had to learn to control my daydreams. Not only would I not do that to Elsa or Karl, but I wouldn't want to waste an ability like magic on crushes. Subbing had shown me there was a lot more to life than boys, a lot more places where others could use help. That's what I'd want to do, if I could. Help people.

And not just royals. Sure, I enjoyed helping out the princesses while I was in Level One, but were all my Level Two jobs going to be like Millie? Did magic really exist so that Millie didn't have to talk to an annoying boy or endure a corset? That job was a long way from the legend of the first Egyptian sub, Woserit. She'd used her magic to save a life. What was Façade's magical purpose now?

When I peeled my foot off the wall, one of my pictures fell down. It was a black-and-white photo of Elizabeth Taylor playing Cleopatra.

She wore a gold headpiece with a beetle on top, the same figure found on the back of Genevieve's calling card. I knew beetles symbolized something, but I couldn't remember what. I thought about looking it up online, but it was late and I'd already been on the computer enough.

Besides, I would only be putting off what I had been putting off all day.

"Okay," I said out loud to my Wall o' Awesome Things. A picture of Karl in his school uniform looked down on me sternly. "So, Genevieve? I'm calling you. Now."

The card on my pillow buzzed, the beetle on the back flashing. I watched it for a few seconds, on guard in case the bug suddenly took flight and attacked me. This is Façade we're talking about. Anything could happen.

When the flashing stopped, my manual made a weird . . . trilling sound. Like an old-fashioned phone. I opened it to the image of a young man with very black skin and very white eyeballs. His features looked computer generated—no one could naturally be that chiseled. He blinked. "You called for Genevieve?" he asked in a clear accent. At first I thought it was British, but it was softer than that. Maybe . . . South African?

I stared at him, trying to place the accent, but also trying to figure out why there was a video of this guy on my manual screen.

"I am Genevieve's secretary, Dominick."

"Hi, Dominick," I said.

Dominick sniffed. "You called for Genevieve. How may I assist you?"

"Oh. Sorry. I'm Desi. She told me to contact her if I had any magical experiences."

"She is in a meeting right now. Is this urgent?"

"Urgent? No. I had play rehearsals today and felt kind of . . . Never mind. I'll try her later."

Dominick held up a finger and pushed on an earpiece with the other. "Yes? Yes, her name is Desi. . . ."

He raised an eyebrow at me.

"Oh. Just Desi." I rushed. "It's not short for anything."

"Last name," he mouthed.

"Bascomb. Sorry."

"Desi Bascomb. Something about a magic play."

He paused, listening to someone on the other end. "Right away, Genevieve."

He glanced up. "I am connecting you to Genevieve. Please be brief. She is very busy. I'm surprised she's talking to you."

His image clicked off, replaced a moment later by Genevieve. She smiled warmly. "Hello, Desi. Did you need to tell me something?"

Suddenly I felt really, really stupid. How could I say that I felt like a fairy today while I was at rehearsal? How lame is that? Genevieve already told me magic didn't happen without the Rouge to activate it, and not outside the confines of Façade. And, of course, that made sense, especially now that I knew all about the history and that royal pact. I'd been so convinced, but now looking at Genevieve, I had some doubts.

"I . . . um . . . I . . ."

Dumb! This was THE HEAD OF FAÇADE. She had to be the busiest woman alive, and here she was taking a moment to talk to a lowly sub, and I couldn't even form a sentence. But what sentence would I form? My reason for contacting her seemed sillier and sillier by the second.

"I'm sorry. I didn't realize this card would contact you directly. I was . . . working on a birthday present for you and the words just came out."

Genevieve shook her finger. "A present? No presents! I'm far too old for such pomp and circumstance."

"Okay."

"I must get back to this meeting, then. Now that you've done . . . let's call this a trial run. You know how easy it is to get a hold of me. If that buzzing feeling you spoke of returns at all, do let me know. Even if it isn't magic, we want to figure out how to differentiate, and, of course, what your triggering emotion is. Are you sure there is nothing else?"

"Positive." I considered mentioning the play, but I was afraid it would make me sound wishy-washy.

Genevieve's image faded, replaced again by Dominick. He looked down at me from over his glasses. "Can I help you with anything else, Miss Bascomb?"

"No. I'm fine. Sorry. Thanks."

"Good day, then."

The screen went blank and I chucked my manual against the pillow. What a colossal waste of time. I shouldn't have been worrying about calling cards and fairy buzzing. Now was the time for me to focus on my play and knock off some of my BEST training.

Now was the time for me to get back to Façade, where the *real* magic happened.

Chapter
11

Ever since Mom and I had had our ice cream girlie fest, we were making an effort to be more involved in each other's lives. At least, the part of my life I could share with her. Over the next three weeks, Mom practiced my lines with me, and sometimes I'd come downstairs and sit in on her Celeste consultations (yes, Celeste, purple is your color, for the gazillionth time). The etiquette and poise involved in the Millie job proved that pageant training could help supplement my BEST. But when Mom asked me to drive up with her to meet Celeste and her mother at the Miss Teen Dream pageant, well, I think my exact words were . . .

"I would rather clean out a hamster cage with my teeth."

"Your dad has a law conference in Reno. I'm not leaving you home alone."

"I'll stay with Kylee."

"And I need help with Gracie."

"So you're not asking me. You're telling me."

"The hotel is nice."

Which was my Mom's way of saying, *You're going. Don't argue*.

The pageant was at the Grove—a fancy downtown Boise hotel that included a banquet hall and theater, so we never needed to leave the building. The reception area paled in comparison to Façade's, but it was the nicest building I'd seen in my real life, much nicer than the Comfort Inns we frequented on family vacations.

After two hours in the car, Gracie had Cheerios sticking to her whole body. I de-cerealized her in the lobby. Celeste showed up and hugged my mom. I thought I'd have another hour with my mom, but Mrs. Juniper had a migraine, so she released Celeste alone into the wild.

Celeste settled into strategizing mode. "It's looking good," she whispered to my mom. "Half these girls have never done a pageant. The city girls are the only real competition."

"Stay positive." Mom furrowed her brow. "The competition is mental. It's not you versus them, it's you versus yourself. And we want you presenting the very best Celeste."

I kissed Gracie's head, trying to stop the laugh tickling my throat. The "best Celeste" would have duct tape over her mouth.

Gracie conked me on the head with her shoe.

"Don't hit. That's bad."

"Bad, bad, bad."

She swung again, and I ducked. "I guess I'll go take her to the indoor pool. Do you want to meet up at all before the pageant?"

"I don't think so," Mom said. "We have the breakfast, the interview, the final walk-through . . . Gracie would be a mess."

"Sure. Well, good luck! I have my cell—" My purse buzzed. I stopped talking and stared at it for a second, trying to make sense of why it would be moving. My cell phone was in my pocket; the only reason I carried a purse now was so my manual and Rouge could be close by. . . .

My manual.

"If it's your dad, tell him we got here fine."

I had to leave. Now. "Right! I need to go to the bathroom, actually, so I'll go talk in there. Uh . . . here, take Gracie." I hoisted Gracie onto Mom's hip. Gracie grabbed for her nose.

"The breakfast starts in a half hour," Celeste said.

"Aren't you going to answer your phone?" Mom asked.

"Yes! Right now. I'll be back. It's not like I can hold her on my lap in there."

"Gross," Celeste said under her breath.

I scurried into the large bathroom. Who would have thought working for the most glamorous agency in the world would involve so many bathroom scenes? I locked myself in a stall, pulled the manual out with shaking hands, and gaped at the new icon on the main page. A text message.

> **Meredith:** Are you ready for a new assignment?

I don't know why a text shocked me so much. The manual had more secretive data than the CIA, but at the same time I wondered why this feature was only being brought to my attention *now*, why Meredith never texted me in the past. It could have majorly saved my butt.

> **Desi:** We have text on this thing?
> **Meredith:** Did you seriously ask me that? OBVIOUSLY.
> **Desi:** Can it wait until tomorrow?
> **Meredith:** You're joking.
> **Desi:** I'm at a beauty pageant right now, babysitting my little sister. One day won't matter, right? You can use the Law of Duplicity somehow. It's not like the French Revolution Part Two is going to start because I couldn't work yet.
> **Meredith:** It's funny. I don't see you, and I almost miss you a teensy bit. Then, two messages and I'm ready to . . . Look, you act like our time services are a convenience. No, we follow a precise magical schedule. I need you now.
> **Desi:** Then why aren't you here? Where's the bubble?
> **Meredith:** You don't need the bubble.
> **Desi:** How else am I going to get to the job? Did you double book your clients?

My manual buzzed again. A picture of Meredith showed up with the words INCOMING CALL. I pushed ANSWER.

"This thing has a *phone?* Why didn't you tell me I could use it as a phone?"

"We just discussed freezing time, and a PHONE impresses you?"

"Why did you text me, then? Why didn't you call? Or do that cool video thing that Gen—"

"Sweet royals! Shut up. I'm trying to save *time*. Here's the deal: this job just came up. It's a watcher position and absolutely perfect for you."

"Perfect? Did I get a request? Is it Elsa?"

"No it's more . . . local than that. That's why you don't need the bubble."

"It's in Idaho? There is a princess in *Idaho?* Meredith, I'm totally confused. Will you tell me what's going on? Oh, man, if there is a costume or a comic-book convention going on—"

"Relax! You don't even need to wear Rouge this time. Desi, you are going to stay *you*. I had a girl pop up on our magic radar, so we're having her do her trial sub for a contestant in your beauty pageant. The contestant, McKenzie, is a pageant veteran but hates it—she only competes because her mom makes her. We've used McKenzie to test subs before because she loves ditching. All you have to do is watch this potential sub and make sure she doesn't do any major damage. You're already there anyway, so it saves us the cost of travel. Works out quite well."

"But isn't there an issue with me being *me*?"

"Unless the girl sets the hotel on fire with a curling iron, you don't have to do anything but observe. You're our security net. It doesn't matter who you are while you're watching."

Making money while sitting through this pageant. Brilliant. I'd probably make more today as a watcher than the winner would make in scholarship money, and I wouldn't have to do that cheesy cry/wave victory walk at the end.

"So when I'm done, I tell you if I think she has princess sub potential?"

"That decision is ultimately up to the council, but you will fill out some paperwork similar to a PPR, should she advance. If she's a disaster, nothing you say matters. Which reminds me, please remember, you are WATCHING, not changing things or impacting!"

The bathroom door opened, and some girls walked in, laughing. I lowered my voice to just above a whisper. "Got it. Send me the info."

"That's what I like to hear—brief and complacent. I'll be back in touch after the pageant. You can text me with emergencies, but don't abuse this feature. We're talking blood, fire, natural disaster—If it would make the nightly news, then call. Best of luck, darling. Ta-ta."

I was about to open the door when the two girls stopped laughing and started gabbing. Walking out then would have been awkward, so I held up my feet and waited.

"Come on, Willow, you know we're going to be finalists. Big counties always are."

"Yeah, I hope so." The sound of water rushing out of the sink, and the hand dryer, blocked some of what the second girl (Willow, I guessed) said. "So many girls are on their game."

"And a million more aren't. Did you see that girl from Fredonia County? Celestial or Angel or something like that. Her tan was so fake and she looked so farm fed."

"Yeah, you're right."

"Does this lipstick look all right?"

"With that shirt, yes, but I hope you aren't using it during evening gown."

"Duh. But I have four different shades for evening gown, so you'll have to help me decide."

The girls laughed again and left the bathroom. I lowered my feet onto the tile. Huh. Usually, I was the girl being made fun of, and Celeste was the one doing it. Still, those girls weren't only insulting Celeste—they were making fun of my hometown. I hoped one of them wasn't the girl I had to watch.

As if in response to my thoughts, my manual buzzed with agency information on Real McKenzie (I didn't need to know anything personal about the sub. She wasn't even supposed to tell me her name). With her round cheeks, chunky glasses, and short hair streaked platinum blond and bright red, McKenzie wasn't your average pageant contestant.

Sub-trial Client: MCKENZIE LIGHTHOUSE, Miss

Sampson County

Age: 14

Basic information provided by agency profiler:

McKenzie was forced to enter pageant by mom. She contacted Façade cover agency for look-alike. (Like all non-royal clients, she's unaware of magical connection— our trial clients foolishly think prosthetics create their mirror image.) Given the fact that McKenzie has been in innumerable pageants and managed to place last in every one but Miss Sampson County (which had only four contestants, three of whom were disqualified after an unfortunate nail polish fight), we're sure finalist is not in her future. Keep an eye on our sub throughout the day. Important that she stays in character, yet doesn't do anything too extreme. McKenzie should not have to face consequences/pageant responsibilities when she returns.

I pushed the stall door open and hurried back, already searching for McKenzie. Perkiness coated the entire lobby. Girls clustered in groups, their sashes over their carefully planned "casual" outfits. I spotted McKenzie across the room, talking to Miss Idaho Falls. McKenzie's outfit took casual to the extreme—navy cords with a hippie-style embroidered shirt. Miss Idaho Falls' eyes kept flitting over McKenzie's clothing, her expression a mixture of shock and disgust. I was trying to make eye contact when my mom squeezed my shoulder. "Here, take Gracie. We need to head over to the banquet hall for the breakfast."

The crowd was thinning out. All I could think about was McKenzie, who would be at the breakfast. I had to *watch* McKenzie. So . . .

"Can I come?" I asked.

Celeste made a face. Mom looked surprised. "To the breakfast? I thought you were taking Gracie to the pool."

"I am. Well, I will. But . . . all I had were Cheerios. And I've always wanted to see this behind-the-scenes stuff. And Celeste's mom isn't going, so I could take her spot, and . . . Please, Mom? PLEASE?"

I held my breath. I noticed Celeste was doing the same thing.

Mom patted my arm. "As long as Gracie is happy, I don't think it'll be a problem. I'm excited you're taking an interest in the program. If I had thought of it beforehand, I would have asked you to make TEAM CELESTE shirts."

Somewhere in Sproutville, my T-shirt design software just cried out in terror.

We followed the stream of girls to the ballroom doors. Mom played patty-cake with Gracie as we waited. Celeste pulled me to the side.

"First you tried out for the play, now you're moving in on my pageant. Stop trying to *be* me."

I kept my face blank. "But Celeste. I already made a TEAM CELESTE shirt. I was going to wear it with our old BFF necklaces."

"See? You're such a follower. I knew you were trying to be my friend again."

"Oh my gosh. It's called sarcasm. Try it sometime."

Celeste flipped her hair and pushed ahead of me.

The hotel brochure featured mostly corporate events, so

it was probably the first time this room was decorated with gold and pink balloons and a POISE, POWER, AND POSITIVITY! banner over the flower-adorned podium. Celeste bounced from table to table, searching for our spot. "I hope we sit by someone decent," she whispered to my mom. "You can learn so much from the veterans."

We found our table at the same time as the girl sitting next to us—McKenzie. Well, Fake McKenzie. Celeste's face fell as she took in her ensemble.

"Hi! I'm McKenzie!" McKenzie gushed. "This is my mom! Isn't this pageant exciting! Where are you girls from?"

Her excitement bordered on manic. Not the tone a bored, anti-pageant girl would take. I lowered my voice, hoping she would adopt the same calm. "I'm Desi. This is Gracie and my mom. And she"—I pointed to Celeste—"is the future queen of the universe. Together, we are Team Celeste."

"I'm from Fredonia County," Celeste said.

"Oh! Cool! Are you all sisters?!"

Celeste and I snorted in unison. McKenzie's mom patted her daughter's hand. "I've never seen you so excited about a pageant. You aren't lulling me into a false sense of security, are you?" She let out a frightened laugh. "Not going to dump pig's blood on the winner, right?"

"What? No! This is great. Oh my gosh, look at the size of this Danish! Have you ever seen a bigger Danish?!"

McKenzie prattled on about how lovely the place settings were, how pretty all the contestants looked. Her mom stared at her like she was an alien. Celeste let out an obvious yawn. I bit into a buttered bagel, thinking as I chewed.

Even though the room looked like Barbie had vomited sparkles, I was excited about this job. Millie's gig had been so cut-and-dried, but this job *mattered*. I knew how wonderful subbing was, and I wanted to make sure Fake McKenzie got the chance to experience Façade for herself. She didn't know it yet, but today had the potential to be one of the biggest days of her life, and it was a treat for me to be a part of that. I needed to be a big part—a kick-this-girl-in-the-pants part—because Fake McKenzie required some serious help.

To begin with, Fake McKenzie's enthusiasm had to be dialed down a notch. So when the lights flashed once to indicate the beginning of the program, I dropped my napkin and dipped down at the same time as McKenzie to pick it up.

"I'm watching you," I said.

"Um, okay."

"No." I shook my head. "I'm *watching* you."

"Wait, you mean like you're—"

"Shhh. I'm going to give you a tip." I lowered my voice. "Don't talk so much. McKenzie doesn't want to be here."

"I know, but I think it's so exciting—"

"It's not about what *you* think, it's what McKenzie thinks."

"Okay. Fine. But did you see that gorgeous tiara ice sculpture?"

"Stop." I pointed at my eyes, then at hers. "Watching. You."

McKenzie bit her lip and nodded. Celeste cleared her throat, and McKenzie and I sat back up.

"Welcome back," said Celeste. "How did your under-the-table-bond session go?"

"Look, girls." Mom passed Gracie over to me and nodded at the front podium. "That's Angie Swiftly. We were in the pageant circuit together. Oh, she's had some work done. Doesn't she look fantastic?"

Angie Swiftly looked like someone had thrown her a surprise party and she'd never let go of the *whoa!* facial expression. The presentation was sixty minutes of positive thinking and encouragement and reach-for-the-stars barf-ness. Everyone smiled. The whole time. Without stopping. While they talked, while they listened. When they were chewing. Even their frowns were smiley. McKenzie smiled the biggest.

I watched her every move, hoping my first trial sub would swallow her giddiness and pass this pageant test.

Chapter
12

Watching is a passive word, but I was anything but passive during the next couple of hours. I alternated between seeing that Gracie was fed/changed/napped and keeping my eye on Fake McKenzie. I couldn't sit through her actual interview—no one but the judges saw that—but I did catch her practicing in the halls.

Which Real McKenzie wouldn't have done.

And I saw her during the dance rehearsal, beaming and boogying with delight.

Again, not Real McKenzie-like.

But the kicker happened less than an hour before the pageant began. Everyone was rushing around backstage, finishing up last-minute preparations. Mom kept hair-spraying

Celeste's spiral curls until, I swear, a tiara-sized hole opened in the ozone layer.

Gracie rubbed her tongue and made a face. "Bad."

"Smart baby."

"Honey, you really don't have to be back here," Mom said. "Again, I appreciate your support, but this is kind of do-or-die right now."

"I have to agree, Mrs. Bascomb. I don't know if she's even *supposed* to be back here."

"Fine. I'll go save some seats. I want to sit right in the front so I can hold up my CELESTE IS MY FAVORITE PERSON IN THE WORLD sign."

"Desi, don't." Mom stuck a bobby pin in Celeste's hair. I looked around one more time for McKenzie. I hadn't seen her since the dance rehearsal. It was prep time, so unless she'd gouged herself with a mascara wand, I figured things were good.

Things were not good. I spotted McKenzie bouncing as Mrs. Lighthouse smoothed down her hair. Her hair that was now devoid of highlights! Fake McKenzie had dyed her hair. *McKenzie's* hair. And the moment Real McKenzie came back, so would her highlights, meaning she'd have to explain the sudden streak switch.

"I'm going to get Gracie a snack before things start."

"Wait, I'm out of bobby pins." Mom cursed under her breath. "Who took all my bobby pins?"

"Uh, I'll see if McKenzie has some." I dodged my way through the crowd until I reached McKenzie. She squealed when she saw me. "Aren't you so excited?! I'm so excited! I love performing. And you should see my evening wear!"

"Seriously, what are you up to, McKenzie?" Mrs. Lighthouse wrinkled her forehead. "Please don't embarrass me. I won't make you do any more pageants, I promise."

McKenzie pecked her mother's cheek. "Don't be silly! I am going to make you so proud!"

"Mrs. Lighthouse, mind if I steal McKenzie away for a second? I, uh, want to give her some smiling pointers."

"You two aren't plotting something, are you?"

"No, ma'am."

"Then, fine." Mrs. Lighthouse waved her hand. "I'm going out 'front to watch. I'm getting too old for this. No tricks!"

I waited until Mrs. Lighthouse was gone, then I grabbed McKenzie's arm. "What did you do to your hair?"

"Bad," Gracie said. *Smart baby.*

"Your sister is so cute! You should put her in a junior pageant, but maybe after she gets more hair."

"She has plenty of hair. And hers isn't highlighted! McKenzie, what were you thinking?"

"Oh, McKenzie isn't my real name. It's—"

"DON'T TELL ME! Don't you get it?" I let out an exasperated breath. One that, yikes, kind of sounded like Meredith. "We aren't talking right now. I'm not helping you."

"You're right. You aren't." McKenzie patted her perfectly poofed hair. "I'm doing fine on my own, just trying to *help* this poor girl. Did you see how awful those highlights were?"

"That's not your job."

"I know. I'm supposed to pretend to be her. But it doesn't hurt to try to help her, right? Haven't you ever done that?"

I dug my fingernails into my palm. Busted. But when I tried to help my subs, I did what they wanted, even if they didn't say it. McKenzie's personality was apparent from the profile, and I was positive she wasn't going to be happy about the dye job. There's impacting, and then there's sabotage.

"Fine. Just . . . tune down your excite-o-meter. Get through this trial job before you try to save the world."

The lights flashed on and off. "Only contestants backstage now. All family and coaches, please be seated."

"Don't worry." McKenzie flashed me a smile. "I'm going to wow them!"

"*Them?*" I called as she hurried away. "You mean your potential employer, right?"

She didn't answer.

The pageant opened with a completely dark stage. The music, slow and dramatic, crescendoed into a flash of pyrotechnics raining over the smiling contestants. The pageant theme song—"Poise, Power, and Positivity!"—cued the girls into their dance, proving how poised, powerful, and positive they were. McKenzie added an extra spin during the second twirl. What was this crazy girl like in her *real* life?

After three minutes, the music quieted and the MC, a

local radio DJ named Danny Dakota, strode over to his podium. I hoped he was getting paid for this. Payment would make his tight tux and pink cummerbund less tragic. "Welcome to Miss Teen Dream Idaho! Introducing this year's contestants."

One by one, the girls sashayed up to the mike. "Hi! I'm Jennifer Frederick from Sun Valley! I love tennis and hope to go to veterinary school someday! Dream big!"

"Hey! I'm Celeste Juniper from Fredonia County. I love puppies and I'm starring in my school play."

I could have pummeled her. Starring? She was a background fairy. Who's trying to be who now?

The introductions hit a steady rhythm, girl after girl, until McKenzie got up.

I longed to use magic then. Or jump into her skin and do this part for her. Anything to give this nameless girl a chance to work at the most awesome job in the world. But I had a different job, as hard as it was. And my job was to watch.

Watch her walk up right to that stand, smile, and say. "Hello! I'm McKenzie Lighthouse from Sampson County. I work with children because I believe they are our future. Also, I love glitter!"

This was not the line she'd said during rehearsal. During rehearsal, she'd said the line McKenzie would have wanted. "I hate fake eyelashes and like free-range, organic chicken!" This children-are-the-future garbage was improvised. I glanced at the judges, seated at the long side table. They were all smiling.

Could I have stopped her? No. There was nothing I

could have done. It was her trial—her choices. I had to watch her make them. Yuck. This was the least impactful job I'd ever had. There had to be a way to do *something*.

The other girls finished their introductions, and Danny Dakota swept across the stage, explaining the criterion for the finalists. He paused dramatically before announcing, "And let's see which eight of these forty-four young ladies we'll be spending time with tonight!"

"First up . . . Celeste Juniper from Fredonia County!"

My mom let out a loud holler. So even though Celeste wasn't my favorite person, I was glad to see that Mom's hard work had paid off. I followed up with a whoop of my own.

The next six names were called—including one of the girls from the bathroom, Willow. And then Danny paused. "One name remains."

The air in the room was sucked out as every girl onstage held her breath.

"The last finalist is . . . McKenzie Lighthouse, Miss Sampson County!"

Not good. So not good. Real McKenzie wouldn't be excited about this! What if her mom expected this to happen again? I had to get backstage and make sure McKenzie didn't win, even if it required something drastic, like evening gown mutilation. Losing this pageant would be an ultimate win for both McKenzies—and for me. If the first sub I watched was a reject, what would that mean for my Façade future? After my trip to the Court of Royal Appeals, I wanted to keep my record free of mistakes and filled with success.

"Mom. I have to go. Bathroom."

I scurried down the aisle before my mom could object. The backstage area was almost flooded with the tears of the non-finalists. I dodged the river of mascara streaks, hoping to sneak into the finalists' changing room, but the stage door was locked, with the sign FINALISTS ONLY. DO NOT SABOTAGE. above it.

It's like they'd read my mind. Still, I faced my dilemma—should I sit back and let Fake McKenzie do her thing, or do I intercede? Was McKenzie's becoming a finalist enough of an emergency to contact Meredith?

It couldn't hurt to text her. Well, this is Meredith we're talking about so it could hurt *a lot*, but it was worth the risk. It wasn't like summoning Genevieve. Meredith could ignore me if she wanted to—she was a pro at that.

Desi: Hey Mer, I have an impact wannabe over here.

My phone rang almost instantly.

"Never call me Mer again."

"It sure got you on the phone quick."

"I'm on the other line anyway."

I bet she was on the line with her prince. I pictured him tapping his fingers as he waited on hold. I wondered what his fingers looked like. I wondered what *he* looked like. Meredith's so petite, it'd be cute if he was short too. They could get a mini-pony together and live in a tiny cottage with animal-shaped shrubs out front. . . .

"Hey. Desi," Meredith snapped into the receiver. "Today."

"Sorry. Fake McKenzie's a finalist—she's in it to win it. And Real McKenzie wouldn't want that."

"Is she physically hurting anyone or blabbing about the agency?"

"They're in a locked room right now, but I doubt it."

"Make sure she doesn't place in the top three. Those girls have to ride on floats and attend events, and our client would not be happy. Finalist isn't the end of the world. Real McKenzie can't complain when she's getting a free trip out of the switch."

"Got it."

"And Desi?"

"Yeah."

"We need to go over what the word *emergency* means."

I found an empty backstage wing, where I had a clear view of the rest of the program. No one besides contestants were supposed to be back there at this point—even moms and coaches were in the audience—but I needed to be close to McKenzie in case she got too pageant peppy again.

Celeste did a monologue from *Our Town* and McKenzie sang "Over the Rainbow" for the talent routine. The sub had lucked out that McKenzie's real talent wasn't instrumental. I knew very well how disastrous that could be (although, actually, disastrous would have been a big help to me at that point). Then the girls did a quick costume change for the final segment—answering interview questions in evening gown.

I'll give her this—Celeste looked amazing in her peach

dress with cap sleeves and a flowy skirt. McKenzie looked pageanty. Her smile was frightening.

The judges' table reminded me of the Court of Royal Appeals, except with more hair spray. A fishbowl filled with interview questions was perched on a column next to the finalists. Danny Dakota swaggered over to the podium, flashing his cheesy smile.

"The first contestant is Miss Georgia Marie Jones from Teton County. Georgia Marie, please pick your question."

Georgia Marie slipped her hand into the fishbowl and handed the sheet of paper to Danny.

"Georgia Marie, If you could take anything with you to a deserted island, what would you take and why?"

Georgia made eye contact with each judge, one by one. "If I were stranded on a deserted island, I would take my country. America is the greatest country on earth, and I believe in life and liberty!"

Danny Dakota swallowed what I could only guess was a snarky remark to such a stupid answer. *My country. Enjoy eighth place, Miss Georgia Marie.*

"Thank youuuuu, Georgia Marie. And God bless America." Danny Dakota shuffled his cards. "Next, Celeste Juniper from Fredonia County."

I knew my mom was proud of Celeste's straight posture as she picked her question and smiled at the judges.

Danny read: "Celeste, do you think our country has a problem with gender bias?"

"Does our country have a problem with gender bias?"

Celeste spoke the words slowly, one of Mom's time-buying tricks. "Well, that's a question I could go on forever about. . . ."

And that's when I saw it. The terror flicker across her face. She had nothing to say. Celeste was about to totally bomb, and I was a firsthand witness.

Three seconds ticked by. Celeste's leg twitched under her skirt.

For how rude Celeste was to me, you'd think I would love her train wreck, but the moment was painful. And not delightfully painful, either, like when you get tickled or eat too much ice cream. This was gouge-your-eyes-out bad. Something welled inside of me, oozing into my heart and my mind and my tear ducts. I would do anything in the world to make the moment end for Celeste.

A smart answer, I thought, would start out: *Yes, our country does have a gender bias, and this pageant is a good example that some things are still viewed as female roles. But at the same time, this pageant includes girls who tomorrow . . .*

My skin and stomach and head and fingers all buzzed. This was the right answer. I knew it. I just needed Celeste to know it.

She was the closest contestant to the curtain. I inched farther out of the wing, as much as I dared, and hissed her name.

She kept her face forward but flicked a quick glance at me. I gave her a thumbs-up sign, and mouthed the word "yes" to get her going. She dipped her chin in the slightest nod and started to speak. When she did, I shook with the intensity of my emotion. Of my . . . magic?

"Yes, our country does have a gender bias, and this pageant is a good example that some things are still viewed as female roles. But at the same time, this pageant includes girls who tomorrow will be our doctors and political leaders. That didn't used to be an option for many women, so in a lot of ways, I feel we've come very far and can celebrate our femininity without forgetting our potential. Thank you."

Celeste's shoulders slumped a fraction as she returned to her stool.

Holy impact miracle! Did that just happen? She gave the exact answer that I was thinking. How did that work? It had to be magic this time, right? Celeste hardly reads books, let alone minds.

I was home, but I was also working for Façade. But I hadn't felt that tingling for my sub; only Celeste. And I wasn't wearing Royal Rouge. So . . . what were the rules here? Was this the "tapping into magical potential" Genevieve had talked to me about? I glanced around at the other finalists to see if they could feel any of the magic that was so obviously thick in the air, but they were busy smiling like coifed crazies. I swung my arms back and forth. I'd impacted in the biggest way yet. Too bad I'd wasted it on Celeste.

From her perch on the stage, Celeste shot me a relieved look and mouthed a thank-you.

So maybe not wasted.

"Next up, McKenzie Lighthouse from Sampson County."

This is great. All I had to do was repeat whatever I did for Celeste, except with a bad answer, and McKenzie would lose. All's well that ends well.

"What are you doing?" A woman dressed in backstage-worker black with one of those headset microphone things pulled me away from the wing. "Are you a contestant?"

"No."

"Then what are you doing back here?"

Danny Dakota read the question. "McKenzie, if you could be anyone else for a day, who would you be and why?"

Oh, sweet irony. But this question was perfect! I started to think of all the possibilities. Um . . . Britney Spears? No, too friendly. Attila the Hun? Too hairy.

"I would be—"

The woman gave me a not-so-gentle push toward the exit door. "I'm calling security if you don't leave now."

I didn't hear the rest of McKenzie's answer, and I couldn't add anything to it now anyway. I felt absolutely no buzzing. No way could I communicate anything to her, especially when I wasn't sure how I was able to communicate to Celeste in the first place.

Watcher fail! Of all the times I should have been there for McKenzie, this was it. A pageant win for Real McKenzie would be a total loss for Fake McKenzie. She wouldn't get to be a sub.

I snuck back into the theater, hoping against all hope that McKenzie's interview did not go well.

Chapter
13

$\mathcal{D}$anny Dakota puffed out his chest. "Ladies and gentlemen, before you stand eight beautiful, talented, and intelligent young women. These poised princesses are the future!"

The crowd applauded.

"Now let's find out who our finalists are. Will the following five contestants please step forward.

"Willow Callaway, Celeste Juniper, McKenzie Lighthouse, Claire Thuet, and Kimi Clow."

The fourth runner-up, Claire, was announced first. Cripes. Whoever Fake McKenzie was, she should go into the pageant world. Her future in the subbing world looked dim.

"The third runner-up, and winner of a five hundred dollar scholarship, is . . . McKenzie Lighthouse."

Fake McKenzie's eyes watered as she took her roses. Her mother, or her fake mother, glanced around the stage, probably wondering when the pigs were going to start flying.

Yes! She didn't place in the top three! Real McKenzie would have no duties to attend to. In fact, she'd come home with decent scholarship money and a happy mother. Sure, things would be changed and Fake McKenzie had gone too far, what with it being a trial gig, but MP is a very special commodity. Not only had Genevieve brought up MP's rarity during lunch, but I remembered hearing about it during Level One training: the agency sometimes went months without picking up anything on their MP radar. So they couldn't be too choosy, right? Fake McKenzie could straighten out during training. Façade had given me a second chance, after all.

"The second runner-up is . . . Celeste Juniper."

Celeste accepted her flowers, her smile staying in the exact position the whole time, just as my mother had taught her. Admittedly, I was relieved. If Celeste had won the whole thing, we would have never heard the end of it.

"And your next Teen Dream Idaho is . . . Willow Callaway!"

Willow wiped at nonexistent tears and took her victory walk. After the music ended, the audience trickled onto the stage. Celeste spotted me and waved before turning to smile at someone else. I didn't have time to think about what it meant—I had to find McKenzie.

Someone grabbed my arm when I stepped backstage. "Hurry. These girls scare me."

"Too positive and poised for you, Meredith?"

Meredith braced herself against a beam. "Don't start."

"So is it over already? I didn't get a text or phone call."

"You probably didn't hear it with all these girls crying. Ugh, all this . . . *emotion* makes me ill."

"Let me say good-bye to our girl."

"Come outside for a moment. We need to talk."

The October air blasted my bare arms as soon as I cracked the back door. We sat down on the stairs, the one lightbulb illuminating the angles in Meredith's expressionless face. "McKenzie is gone."

"You mean Fake McKenzie?"

"Yes. The sub."

"Oh." The icy wind licked my skin. Meredith didn't so much as shudder in her chic sleeveless turtleneck.

"Is she going to the agency now?"

"She'll have a quick stop at the agency, yes."

I sighed. "You don't know how relieved that makes me. Watching is so hard, like you can't *do* anything. It's the opposite of subbing."

"Well, the opposite of your subbing style, Miss Impact," Meredith said.

"I'm glad she did enough to make it through. Are you going to do her Level One training, or is someone else on that?"

"Desi. She's going to the agency to get sub sanitized."

A chill ran through me that had nothing to do with the

weather. What I knew about sub sanitization wasn't pretty—all memory of Façade was wiped away. If I hadn't been cleared of charges by the Court of Royal Appeals, I would have faced the same fate. I couldn't imagine knowing about Façade, about all of this, and then going back to regular life, unaware that this world even existed. "Why would they . . . why would they do that?"

"Because she didn't *pass*. We don't want her bringing home memories as a souvenir." Meredith snapped open her clutch and popped a Tic Tac in her mouth. "You want one?"

I pushed away her outstretched hand. "Wait, so she's just done? That's it?"

"Yes. It's a trial." She closed her purse. "Some pass. Most don't."

"I can't believe this." I rubbed my hands up and down my arms. "I feel like a failure."

"Hey, you did your job fine. You watched. You can't *make* someone act a certain way. If you could, you and I wouldn't have half the problems we do, would we?"

"You seriously aren't hiring her? She was just excited; that would wear off soon. She had a caring heart. And throwing a girl into a beauty pageant? That's ridiculous."

"A lot of things you subs are asked to do are ridiculous. That's the point of a trial. We put you into the situation to see if you are able to solve problems and think on your feet. You handled your trial fine. I passed mine. It happens, not very often, but that's how we know we have the brightest and best."

"So that's it. She's gone."

"Adios. And let's not dwell too long on this. I have enough going on back at Façade. Lilith is on a rampage, brownnosing anyone and everyone who might get her promoted. It's all I can do to keep my hat in the ring. And they're planning games for Genevieve's birthday. *Games*. If Specter wins the trophy for the three-legged race this year, those meatheads will throw it in our face—"

"Stop it!" I threw my hands in the air. "You act like you don't even care about Fake McKenzie."

"Ah, I forget how sensitive you are. Do you know how many girls I've seen fail their trial? Dozens. And good riddance to them—if we took them into the agency, they would be a risk. She won't even remember the pageant happened. Especially once her magic potential is gone."

"What do you mean 'her magic potential is gone'? Where does it go?"

Meredith stood and brushed off her gray slacks. "You're being silly about this. It's not your problem. You should get back, find your mom, and I'll see you as soon as your training is—"

"You can't . . . You don't take MP *away* from her, do you?"

"We're doing the sub—society—a favor." Another gust of wind blew a plastic bag onto Meredith's foot. She looked down and it floated away. Even inanimate objects were intimidated by her. "We used to only take away memory, not MP. Big mistake. Façade's history is speckled with rejects who misused magic. There was one woman—Jericho—who

139

was fired when we learned she'd stolen her clients' jewels for years. Once home, Jericho became one of the most notorious thieves in the world—she could walk into a bank and convince them to give her whatever she wanted; no one knew how she did it. We suspect she remembered enough about Façade to channel her MP—which was still there. So don't get self-righteous on me. Trust me, Fake McKenzie isn't going to miss her MP. It's a responsibility best left for those who know how to handle it."

"Genevieve told me that all these weird feelings I'm having at home have nothing to do with magic, because magic only happens for a sub when she has on Rouge. So once this Jericho was home, her magical past shouldn't have mattered. She must have been a sneaky thief. Her crimes and her magic weren't related."

"It matters. And I find it hard to believe that *you* believe otherwise." Meredith pointed her phone at the ground, and her bubble quivered out. She didn't look at me when she spoke again. "I've said enough. I'll be in touch soon."

"No! I want some answers."

"Then figure out the right questions, darling. Ta-ta."

I jerked the backstage door open and slammed it behind me. Contestants glanced up from their conversations, the area quiet.

"Sorry. Needed fresh air."

I tried to get down the side stairs and out of the theater without being noticed, but my mom saw me and waved. "Desi! Where did you go?"

"I had a backstage pass."

"Here. Take Gracie back to the room. Celeste has press photos."

Gracie rested her head on my shoulder and yawned. I carried her to the elevator and pounded the button with my thumb. McKenzie and her mom hardly noticed when the doors dinged open and Gracie and I squeezed inside. Mrs. Lighthouse was analyzing her daughter's hair, which was back to funky highlights.

"I still don't understand how your highlights came back so quickly," Mrs. Lighthouse said.

"I told you, they were temporary."

"But you haven't even washed your hair."

"New formula. Who cares—let's talk about something more important. How I was in the top five? I wasn't supposed to be in the top five." McKenzie scowled at her roses like they were weeds. "What a rip-off."

"You were captivating tonight." Mrs. Lighthouse fanned her hand in front of her face like she was about to cry. "I think you're ready to hit the competitive circuit hard."

"The only thing I'm hitting hard is that girl's face."

Mrs. Lighthouse went on like she hadn't heard her daughter. "And I'm so proud that you didn't do anything obscene. I didn't hear one curse the entire time you were onstage."

"I was saving those for later." The elevator stopped on their floor. McKenzie chucked her roses on the ground and stomped out.

Gracie lifted her head and pointed at the roses. "Bad?"

I kissed her forehead. Smart baby.

When I got to my room, I tucked my sister into bed and noticed that Kylee had texted me: Did any of the beauty queens turn into werewolves?

I wished Kylee was at the pageant. I needed someone, or something, to distract me from my thoughts. No matter how hard I tried, I couldn't push away Meredith's always confusing answers.

There were clearly things I didn't know about Façade and magic. I wanted to believe that everything was as clean and glamorous as the agency's reception area, but now that Fake McKenzie hadn't made it, I was starting to notice the spots.

If the story Meredith told me was true, then magic could be used anywhere. I didn't need to be on Façade's clock. I didn't need the Rouge. Even before I'd started working with Façade, I'd had twinges of bigness, and now they'd escalated during play rehearsals. So magic was there, in me. Somehow.

By why would Façade lie? Was their reason really to stop me from stealing jewelry or taking over the world? Meredith said it was a protection, but Façade put subs in harm's way all the time—volatile bubbles, sticky royal situations. I mean, royals can be *assassinated*. So if they trusted me enough to hire me, trusted me with the huge secret that Façade even existed, then why not explain the full capacity of magic?

It's not like I thought Façade was evil or anything. And

everyone besides Lilith had been gracious and kind. Even Meredith, underneath her Coat of Snarky Colors, was honest and caring. It was more like there was a piece to the puzzle that I was still missing.

Façade tried to control magic to the point that they took it away if they didn't like how it was used . . . took it away without the poor girl's consent. They didn't own some magical monopoly—it was clear that magic existed beyond the Rouge and bubbles and royals. Suddenly, it dawned on me. Genevieve knew this, and that's why she'd given me her card—so she could *monitor* me. Well, now I knew better. I would keep my experiences to myself.

And figure out how to have more magical moments.

Chapter

14

I spent a lot of time alone in my room over the next two weeks. My mom asked if the pageant had somehow upset me, if I needed to talk. I *did* need to talk, but there was no one to talk to. The people in my home life couldn't know anything about Façade. And the people at Façade—well, I wasn't sure who I could talk to there anymore.

There were two ways for me to find answers. The obvious one was to get back on another job. So I researched, researched, researched. Fashion spreads, yacht blueprints, basic sewing skills. And when I wasn't doing that, I was preparing for the play. I'd felt the buzzing twice while rehearsing. To understand that magic, I had to figure out what sparked it.

We were only two weeks away from opening night, so by now everyone was comfortable with their lines and the scenes were blocked. Now it was more about our facial expressions and hand gestures. The *nuances*, as Mrs. Olman would say. She pulled me aside once and mentioned that I should try to "connect" like I did during auditions. The fact that she could sense my lack of magic only frustrated me more.

And, oh! I didn't even need to worry about the kiss. Reed had to wear a DONKEY HEAD. Like a legitimate costume head. Mrs. Olman ordered it from a specialized Shakespeare costume company. Which sounds impressive, but the thing was hideously massive. The first rehearsal he had to wear it, I was so glad I was a fairy. Well, I was glad for that regardless—I'd helped the costume team with a few design ideas, hoping it would count toward my BEST. They did this cool beadwork thing that twisted all around the skirt of my costume so it caught the stage lights and sparkled.

But Reed? He looked ridiculous. Which was the point. It still made it hard to block the scene, since he wasn't used to the costume's weight.

"You need to overexaggerate your movements," I whispered to him as Mrs. Olman showed the servant fairies how to flutter (including Celeste, who needed a little humility now that she'd told everyone she was *practically* Miss Teen Dream Idaho). "You don't have your face to convey the meanings."

Reed jerked his head to the side, so I assumed he was

staring at me. "And what experience do *you* have wearing a donkey head?"

"I don't. But I do have plenty of mascot experience from my old job at a pet store, and I know how heavy that thing can get. You don't want the audience to know that. It's supposed to be your real head now. Whatever magic changed you probably also gave you sturdy neck muscles."

"And what do you know about magic?"

Ha. Hahahahahaha. HA. "Hey, I took your advice. No need to bite my head off just because yours is so inflated now."

The fairies swirled around us. Mrs. Olman clapped her hands in beat. "Counts of eight, girls! It's a dance. And don't chew gum, Celeste!"

"Sorry." Reed pulled off his head. "I wasn't trying to be a jerk. I usually feel a lot more natural when I'm trying to be someone else."

"I think it's funnier if you're awkward."

"Awkward. I got that down, then." He rubbed his staticky hair. "Hey, so I saw your friend Kylee yesterday at the gas station."

I knew this. Of course I knew this. Kylee had called to replay every moment of the two-minute interaction, down to the candy bar he was buying. She'd set a new record by saying ten words to him. At this rate, they would complete an entire conversation by college.

"Oh really? Cool."

"I was thinking . . . we should all hang out sometime."

146

I tried to ignore the teeny thrill I got when he said that. I liked Reed. Not *liked* liked, but I always looked forward to joking around with him at rehearsals. I didn't know how I would have survived the play without him. It could be fun to spend more time with him. With Kylee, of course.

"Would you mind?" he asked. "I'm still new here and I've been so busy working that I haven't gotten to know the real Sproutville."

"You've seen the gas station. That's a major highlight."

Reed played with a donkey ear. "They do have good doughnuts there."

"Sure. Kylee would love it. . . ." I paused. Oops. Didn't want her to sound like she liked him *too* much. Even if she did. "And so would I. We both would. We'll show you the cool, secret places."

"Cooler than Mark Twain's house?"

"Oh, yeah."

"Actors!" Mrs. Olman called out, her voice echoing in the theater. One of the girls in my fairy court looked near tears. "We are not *feeling* things today. We are not reaching out *or* in. I want everyone to sit down on the stage right now."

Everyone shuffled in place. No one sat.

"Now!" Mrs. Olman bellowed.

The floor creaked as we did one obedient plop. "You." Mrs. Olman pointed at me. "Desi. Come stand by me."

I shot a look at Reed. He was trying to cover a smile with his hand.

"Make haste, please. You can make eyes with your donkey boy in a moment."

I could feel my face flame as I stood and joined Mrs. Olman. Making eyes? With Reed? Whatever. Telepathically agreeing that this woman should be head counselor at Camp Crazy Sauce was *not* making eyes.

"Tell me, Desi, have you ever been in love?"

The rest of the cast snickered. "Um . . . I'm only thirteen. Almost fourteen."

"Not quite fourteen. The same age as Juliet, one of the most tragic heroines in the theater."

"Tragic because she was crazy," I mumbled.

"What's that? This is the theater. Speak up."

"It's just . . . Juliet killed herself because of some stupid boy that she'd only known for, like, a week. I wouldn't count that as love."

"You haven't answered the question."

I ducked my head. "Well, I've liked boys. Of course." I thought of Karl. Of course I thought of Karl. But I could easily recognize that my twisted feelings for him were not a Shakespearean tragedy. I hardly knew the guy. I wouldn't kill myself for him. And I was ONLY THIRTEEN. If Juliet was my age when all that Romeo stuff went down, then she was a moron. I was old enough to recognize that I was still too young to claim eternal love. Liking someone? Crushes? That's more my speed. "But I'm no Juliet."

"That's the point. You need to *become* her. You all do. You need to take your own emotional experience, even if it's not nearly as strong as your character's, and pull it out to full strength. I doubt any of you have been jealous enough to kill, like Othello. But the root of that emotion is the same. Play it up in your head. Feel, feel, feel. Now, Reed, come over here, please. With the donkey head."

Reed made a big show of placing his head back on, bumping into me like he couldn't see. "Now. Miss Bascomb. Close your eyes. Think of a boy you like. Capture his image in your head. Got it?"

I closed my eyes, the image of Reed's donkey head replaced by Karl in the garden. "Got it."

"Now, keep your eyes closed. Tell that boy how you feel, but direct it to Reed."

"I wish . . ." I pried open one eye. Reed's donkey face looked down on me. I stifled a giggle. "I wish you liked me the same way I like you."

"There is no emotion in that!" Mrs. Olman kicked the air. "Try again."

I sighed. My one shot to talk to Karl again. What would I say?

The whole cast was watching me, waiting for me to deliver. Time for me to pull that magic out of my hat. Right now. Abracadabra. Any day.

Karl, I love you. No. *Karl, I like you.* No. The words weren't working with Karl. Probably because I knew I could never say those things to him. Not as me.

Karl's face faded and all I saw was Reed. I pictured the face he was making underneath the donkey head—he had to be smiling. He was always smiling. And his eyes probably were crinkly on the side. And he might be licking his lip. He always did that right before he said something funny, like he wanted to taste the deliciousness of the words before he said them. And then I felt a faint spark, a sparkle really, right in my toes—

Wait. Where did *that* come from?

I blinked until the image was gone, losing any concentration I had going for me. There was no swelling or bigness or lovesick devotion. There was nothing. No magic. No feelings. No thinking about the lips of my best friend's crush. That *so* did not just happen.

I realized I still had to deliver a line. I cleared my throat and said, "Er . . . I like you a lot."

Mrs. Olman threw her hands in the air. "No! You need to work on that. Emote, emote, emote."

I swallowed and nodded, worried if I said something, my voice would crack.

"Now, Reed. What about you? Have anyone in mind?"

"I'm not the one in love here, right? I mean, besides in love with myself."

"Have you ever known someone like that, then?"

"I've known a million someones like that."

"Well then, FEEL."

Reed delivered his line. He sounded pompous, self-centered, and likeable. He was more Bottom than any actor had ever been. It was perfect.

"Bravo. Now, Desi, I want you to kiss Reed right on

his donkey lips. Just like you would your love."

"I said I'm not in lov—"

"Fine. Your schoolboy crush. Whatever. Kiss Reed like that. Ignore the fur."

I leaned in and planted one right on his fake lips. The cast giggled. I stroked an ear. The cast laughed. Well, if I can't get magical, at least I can be comical.

Mrs. Olman pointed at the fairies. "See that? That is acting. You two take a seat. Demetrius. You're next."

Reed tugged off his donkey head. "What's up with you? You can do better than that."

"I was fine." I stared straight ahead.

"But you can do better than fine."

I finally looked at him and frowned. "Who's the director here?"

"I'm just saying what Mrs. Olman did at first."

"Maybe I should listen to *Mrs. Olman*."

"You're getting upset because you know I'm right." He wrinkled his forehead. "You aren't trying hard enough."

"Trying? Trying?" I stood up. The rest of the cast was watching me now, but I didn't care. "All I do is *try*. Sorry we can't all be perfect actor boy all the time. Some of us aren't as good at lying as you are."

"Acting isn't lying. It's showing the truth."

"Fine. You're good at it and I'm not."

"That's not what I said. Don't go junior high on me."

Ouch. I *was* being childish, but I didn't care. Besides, being mad at Reed was a lot easier than being . . . whatever

I was being before. And why did that little zing in my toes, the first bit of magic I'd felt since coming home, drain away so quickly? Where was my control? I needed someone to explain how the stupid power *worked*.

"I *am* in junior high. Sorry if I'm not as mature as you."

"Desi, I'm sorry. I was honestly trying to help."

"Well, don't. No, if you want to help, stop telling me what to do." I turned on my heel and walked backstage. I stayed back there until rehearsal was over, then zipped out to my mom's car before Reed got a chance to confuse me any more.

Chapter
15

After the head-kissing weirdness, I kept my distance from Reed, only interacting when necessary during rehearsal. I didn't need any more acting tips or character analysis or mixed-up thoughts. I especially didn't need to spend alone time with my best friend's crush.

Besides, there was the new BEST item to stress over. Real live princesses might not play the parts we see in fairy tales, but they also didn't do this. It had to be a mistake.

The text I received from Meredith simply said: Hey, add roller-skating to your BEST. Trust me.

ROLLER-SKATING.

Although I hadn't used all of the skills I was assigned to learn for Millie, I could see how they could be useful for a sub. I'd traveled to four different countries, and not once had I seen a royal on wheels. Still, it beat the heck out of the minuet, so I figured, mistake or not, I'd try it. Better still, Kylee didn't think it was strange when I asked her to go with me. It was actually the most normal request I'd yet made.

Mrs. Olman had held an early dress rehearsal Wednesday night, giving us Thursday off to *clear our minds*. What better way to do that than to roll up (zing!) to the elementary school's PTA skate night? Kylee and I could be total dorks and not worry about who was there or the fact that we couldn't skate. It was all giggling fifth and sixth graders anyway.

Crystal Palace was bumping. We rented our skates and sat on a bench to lace them up. When I tried to stand, Kylee grabbed my wrist. "I've never done this. Maybe we should get some nachos instead."

"Everyone has to try it sometime." I planted the brake of my skate so I wouldn't wobble. "Just make sure the kids don't plow into you when you fall down."

"And tell me exactly why you've jumped from the violin to roller skates?" Kylee triple-checked her laces.

"Because if I fail at this, I'm only hurting myself. My violin playing hurt everyone, or at least their ears. And it's fun." Fun for an unknown, fashion-savvy princess. The music stopped and the DJ called for skaters ages eight and under to line up for races. A guy in a referee uniform skated to the middle of the rink and blew a whistle at a kid trying to push to the front. When the ref caught me watching him, he waved.

I ducked my head. "You know what, you're right. This is dumb. We'll grab some nachos and go home."

"I was kidding. We already paid."

"I'll pay for you," I said. "I'll pay you to leave right now."

"What's the—" Kylee noticed the ref and her face colored. "Desi. Don't look now, but you'll never guess who the referee is."

"Gee. I bet I can."

"It's Reed."

I shot another quick look at him. His whistle was still between his lips.

I will not think about his lips. "Oh, is it?"

"So we go all summer without seeing him, and he was *here* the whole time? I wish I knew—I could have planned." She smoothed down the baby hairs around her forehead. "I'm a mess. And I can't even skate! What should we do?"

"Leave?"

"No way. This is fate telling me to buck up. If I can't do this now, then it's a sign."

"Sign of what?"

"That I'm wasting my time. If I can't talk to the boy, why bother? I never have a problem talking to other people. I'm not going to have a shallow crush like you did on Hayden." She reached over and squeezed my knee. "No offense."

"Hey." I slapped her hand. "There is something to be said for shallow crushes."

"Not on unshallow boys. Seriously, though. This is

great." Kylee found lotion in her purse and started lathering it onto her hands. "Now, do I have anything in my teeth?"

Reed blew his whistle and the music cranked up while the first age group raced around the rink. Reed skated over to a frustrated boy who kept flopping over. He whispered in the kid's ear and took his hand. They crossed the finish line together.

Kylee fidgeted with her shirt. I tried to stay calm too. This was the first time I'd seen Reed in non-play world since my blowup. I could tell my distance confused him, and probably hurt him. He even tried to talk to me about it once, but when I acted like nothing was wrong, he got the hint and kept our relationship light and casual. Sometimes I'd slip and make a joke, but mostly we were back to where we had been on the day of the audition. Which was good. I didn't need him critiquing my every move. Or being a know-it-all. Or standing so close that I could smell that clean Reed scent of ocean and soap.

When the races ended and the dance music started again, Reed skated to the edge of the rink and leaned over the guardrail. "First you hardly talk to me at rehearsals, and now you're *stalking* me at work?"

"No." I ran my hand along the railing. "I didn't know you worked here."

"Yeah, ever since my family moved to Sproutville last June."

Kylee opened her mouth like she was going to make a

comment, but clamped it shut. Fate wasn't being kind to her yet.

"I never see anyone I know at work, unless they're picking up a little brother or something," Reed said. "So this is perfect! Are you two big skaters?"

Kylee looked down at her rented skates. "I've actually never roller-skated before."

"Seriously? It's a breeze. Want me to teach you?"

"Um . . ." Kylee drew out the um forever, her face going pink. "Yeah. Yes. That would be great."

Reed held out his hand, and Kylee edged onto the rink. She turned back to smile at me, her face flushed and anxious. Reed led her away, one hand holding hers, the other waving animatedly as he spoke. I watched for a second, happy that Kylee was finally getting her chance to talk to Reed, happier still that I wasn't. Then I pictured myself with a tiara on my head and a dress flowing around my skates, and set off to master roller-skating for my secret royal client. I circled around and around the rink, gaining speed and confidence as I went along.

Three laps later, Kylee zipped past me, right into the wall.

"Ow!" she yelled as she rolled onto her back, her legs straight up in the air like three-day-old roadkill. "Ow!"

Reed and I raced over. He kneeled down next to her. "I'm so sorry! Your hand slipped right out of mine."

Kylee moaned. "Lotion."

"Which part hurts?" Reed asked.

"The body part. All of it. Ow!"

I rolled up her pant leg to check the damage. "Well, you're bleeding a little. How does your head feel? Why did you go all Speed Racer?"

"My head's fine. Help me up." Reed and I hoisted her into a sitting position. She slumped against the wall. "I told Reed I wanted to go faster. My fault."

"No, I should have held on tighter. It was like that scene in *Titanic*, when the guy lets go and he drowns in the ocean."

"Except *you* let *her* go." Some teacher. Kylee could have a concussion or internal injuries now.

"I can take you in the back if you want," Reed said. "There's a first-aid kit."

"Thanks. But I'm fine."

"No, you aren't. Hey, it's my job to help. Let me at least get you a drink—" Reed startled a bit, and the smile faded from his face. He stood quickly and ran his hand through his hair. "I have to go."

"Go where?" I asked.

"Go work."

"You just said helping Kylee is your job." I looked around. "And she's the only one on the ground right now."

"Thanks for pointing that out." Kylee rubbed her shins.

"That's what I mean." Reed was already rolling away. "I'm going to get her a drink. Be back."

"Aren't you going to help her up?" I called, but Reed

disappeared into the skate rental room. I looked back at Kylee. "Not exactly a knight in shining armor, is he?"

"He saved your life. Guess I wasn't in distress enough. Or maybe my roller-skating skills repulsed him and he had to flee."

"That was weird," I said. "He's weird."

"No, he's not. Don't talk about him like that. Pull me up." Kylee skirted the wall until she reached the opening and clopped over to our bench. She eased down and moaned. "I'm going to be so sore tomorrow. I get to choose what we do next time we hang out, okay?"

"I'm sorry. I thought this would be fun. Anything you want."

"Zombie movie. No, zombie *marathon*."

"I'll wear my sunglasses so you don't see me sleeping through it."

"Sleep? How can you sleep through the apocalypse?"

I skated over to the bathroom and wet some paper towels to clean up her scratches. I knelt down in front of her bleeding left knee. She winced as I dabbed.

"Reed should be doing this. Where's Mr. First Aid now?"

Kylee was quiet for a few seconds, her expression thoughtful. She finally leaned down and whispered. "Desi. Do you like him?"

"Reed?" I stopped mid-dab. "Are you kidding me? What makes you say something crazy like that?"

"Because you two talk like you've known each other forever."

"We're in a play together."

"You hit it off the first time you met."

"That's ridiculous." I crumpled up the paper towel. "We're friends. Actually, when he gets all bossy, we aren't even that."

"I'm just saying maybe you're a better match for him. He talked the whole time we skated, and I froze. Like usual. I'm not myself with him, and it's stupid."

"Give it time."

"I still think he's cute. And sweet."

"And funny," I added.

"See?" she said softly. "You do like him."

"No, I promise I don't. I like someone else."

"Like that prince."

I nearly choked on my gum. Karl? SHE KNEW ABOUT KARL? How? Did I leave my manual somewhere, or had I let his name slip by accident. . . .

"He's all over your Wall o' Awesome Things. Maybe I should have a celebrity crush too."

I wiped at my forehead. Deep breaths, Desi. Kylee knew I liked Karl. She had no clue I *knew* Karl. Secret's safe. And as for all this Reed stuff, well . . . that was . . . well, it was . . . ridiculous. That's what it was.

The rental room door clicked open and Reed skated out, his hair messy. He was all apologies when he saw us. "Sorry, girls! A referee's job is never done."

"I thought you were getting Kylee a drink."

"I am! Had to check on the foot spray situation.

Disturbing stuff. I'll save you the details. Since you were so patient, I'll finagle you some nachos. Here, be right back."

"Nachos? He thinks *nachos* makes up for leaving you stranded?" I asked Kylee.

"Don't go drama, Des."

Reed came back with three drinks and soggy, cheesy chips.

"Thanks," Kylee said.

The loud dance music faded out, replaced by an eighties love song. "Fellas, grab your ladies. It's couple skate time." The DJ pointed at Reed from inside the booth.

Reed rolled his eyes. "I have to do this. One of you girls want to save me from giggling ten-year-olds?"

"No way am I going out there again." Kylee swallowed a nacho. "Have Desi do it. She still owes you for saving her life."

I shot Kylee a glare. So *now* she could suddenly talk? The last thing I wanted was to couple skate with Reed. It gave him four minutes to critique my performance at dress rehearsal last night. "I'm not a great skater either."

"It's easy."

"Have fun talking!" Kylee held up two chips and smooshed them together like they were kissing. It'd been a while since I'd had a best friend, but this still seemed like a mixed signal. She'd passed me thousands of Kylee <3s Reed notes, and now she was pushing me to couple skate with him?

We wheeled onto the floor. I kept my arms crossed while

Reed held his out. "Uh, we're supposed to touch. Like we're dancing. But skating. I'll be the one going backward. I know it's lame."

I placed my hands lightly on his shoulders. He put his on my waist, but you still could have fit a continent between us. We started moving, not dancing exactly. The silence lasted half a lap around the rink. As much as Reed got to me, the quiet was even worse. "So do you like living in Sproutville?" I finally asked.

"She speaks!"

"Funny."

"Yeah, I like small towns." Reed looked down at his skates. "We lived in New York when I was nine, and I hated that."

"I thought you were from New Zealand."

"I am, but I've traveled all over the world. My parents are doing a ten-year study on the effects of air quality on agriculture, so this is my sixth school. Third country."

"Did you ever think you'd be working at a roller-skating rink in Idaho?"

"It's not the pet store, but the nachos are decent."

When I readjusted my hand on his shoulder, he pulled me in closer. Just a bit.

"How did you know I worked at the pet store?" I asked.

"Oh, when I uh . . . helped you out of the dunk tank last summer. Weren't you doing that for the pet store? And you mentioned it during rehearsals, when I had my donkey head on. Right?"

"Yeah." I gave Reed a point for paying attention. So he was listening in between all his staring and directing. "But I quit. I've got some other things going on."

"Like?"

I'm a magical princess substitute. You? "I design T-shirts and stuff."

A group of girls waved at Reed as they passed us. He graced them with a smile but then turned his attention back to me. We'd done our first lap and the song was about to hit the chorus.

"Yeah, this job's just temporary for me," Reed said.

"What do you want to do?"

"Don't laugh, but I really do want to be an actor. Like, live theater." He shook his head. "Stupid, huh?"

"No." The chorus of the song got loud, and we stopped talking for a bit, wheeling around in our rigid positions. I cleared my throat when the music quieted. "And you know you're a good actor."

"Really, you think so?"

"Reed, you know so."

Reed pursed his lips together. "You think I'm bigheaded, don't you?"

"Not bigheaded. Donkeyheaded."

"Ha-ha." He moved his hands a little lower on my back. "Here's the thing: I'm confident about some things, sure. I've been acting for a long time, and I've had a lot of different roles. So I'd better be good at it by this point."

"So you *do* think you're good."

"Yes! You have to believe in yourself to be great. That's what I keep trying to tell you. Sometimes, when you say a line, it's the most genius thing ever. I'm completely convinced that you're that character, that you understand her. But other times you're just saying words."

"You're seriously going to start directing me?" I tried to pull my hands away, but Reed tightened his grip.

"I'm sorry. I'm messing up again, aren't I?"

"Whatever. It's fine."

"No, this happened last week and you stopped talking to me. I want things to be right between us." He looked away for a bit, considering his next words, then looked me right in the eye. "I can tell you're different, Desi. That's all. And I don't think I've ever met a girl so . . . I don't even know how to describe you. So . . . special."

I almost interrupted him with a joke or a subject change, but he was so earnest, and a part of me—most of me—wanted to hear the rest.

"I hardly know you, but I kind of feel like, in a weird way, I've *always* known you." He blushed. "I'm not trying to confess my undying love or anything. I just want you to know where I'm coming from. I see . . . something, so I might be hard on you because I know there is more there."

"Oh. Um . . . oh."

My stomach knotted. Where did that all come from? I'm not different. Sure, I have magical abilities, but in Idaho I was just Desi. I was content with that. So what was Reed seeing that no one else was? He did say one thing right—he didn't know me.

And holy roller-skates, what was he doing telling me this stuff?

"This is the longest song in the history of couple skating," Reed said. We did one more lap around the rink in silence, and let go quickly when the music ended.

"Kylee probably ate all the nachos by now," I said. Kylee was wrong about the fate thing—just because you can't talk to a guy and he makes you feel sick to your stomach and you don't act like yourself around him . . . that doesn't mean it's a waste of time. Time is exactly what she needed. And I should have stopped Reed when he was saying all that stuff about me.

Except . . . except I didn't want to. "Thanks. For the dance."

"Uh-huh. And, uh, sorry I went off on you like that." Reed fiddled with his ref whistle. "I'll see you tomorrow at the play. Don't break a leg before you break a leg."

"I'd say that to you, but you seem to have this figured out."

He flicked me one more look. "There's a lot I don't have figured out."

His shoulder brushed mine as he skated away, leaving a sharp zap of unexplainable *electricity*.

Chapter 16

When I got to the theater the next night, an hour before curtain, everyone backstage was abuzz with chaotic energy. Mom did my hair and stage makeup at home, so all I needed was to put my costume on and try to not get stage fright. Try.

I found a folding chair next to the sound booth. My lines played over and over in my head. I had a nightmare the night before where I'd forgotten the words. No, actually I'd replaced them with things I'd said while on my subbing jobs. Celeste had laughed and Reed threw his head off and stormed off the stage, leaving me alone in the spotlight.

I shook my head. I didn't have time to analyze the dream—I needed to mentally prepare myself for this moment, a moment I'd thought about as I'd watched the old screen sirens in my favorite movies. I was a legitimate actress, and unlike when I subbed, people would actually know *I* was performing. There was no Rouge to cover up a mistake.

A couple of techies ran past me, both frenzied. "I don't know where he put his head. If I knew, we wouldn't be looking for it."

"How do you lose a donkey head?"

"I didn't lose it. Stop blaming me."

"The play starts in thirty minutes."

"STOP BLAMING ME!"

I swallowed a smile. Reed probably hid the head in the dressing room just to mess with the poor girls. Because, really, that head weighed ten pounds. Hard to miss.

The duffel bag at my feet began to rumble. I zipped it open, but sat back up when I saw my manual light up. Really? Now? We were past the thirty-minute house call. That buzz had better be another BEST instruction and not gig info.

The manual's phone vibration grew louder, causing the duffel bag to inch across the floor.

"Ugh! Be quiet." I yanked the manual out and clicked on the text.

Meredith: Be there in two.

No way. That princess could wait three hours. These

people could stop time! Or slow time town—I don't know how it worked, but whatever was going on at Façade was not as important as my play. Plus, I had to get into character— Titania's character.

Before I could even pound a text of protest, Meredith's bubble popped up.

"I can't go now!" I hissed at the bubble.

The bubble didn't reply.

"Can I at least change?"

Nothing. Not that bubbles talk back, but Meredith could hear me. Her silence said enough. After a minute-long standoff, another text appeared.

Meredith: It's not like I showed up in the middle of the play. You're still fine.

I stomped my foot. "I helped hand-glue a hundred beads onto this costume. I don't want to lose even one while we are in transit."

Meredith stepped out, her hand on her hip. No one else could see her, just me yelling at nothing. But with theater people, talking to the air was a regular event.

"I'm going to yank all those beads off if you don't get going," Meredith said. "My personal time is about to start."

"So that's why you're here on the biggest night of my life?"

"Being at Façade's disposal is what you signed up for, darling. Acting in a theatrical production was your final

BEST accomplishment. Technically, I should have waited until after the play, but I got clearance now. Delivering you to your job is the last thing on my to-do list before I go on vacation."

"You never go on vacation."

"*Exactly*. So I'd like to use the time I have to full advantage. Get inside and check your manual. You're going to have plenty of performance practice with this girl anyway."

I hesitated, and my hesitation was what did me in. Meredith's smile was smug when I entered the bubble, but I refused to give her the satisfaction of admitting that, regardless of the lousy timing, I was dying to find out about this mysterious royal. I flopped onto the couch with my manual and compact, sweeping on some Rouge before clicking on the new profile.

FLORESSA CHASE

Age: 16

Hometown: Hollywood Hills, California

Favorite Book: *Design: A Photo History*

Favorite Food: White cheddar rice cakes. The chocolate ones if I'm being naughty.

Anything Else We Should Know: Like being me isn't awesome enough, I found out about your little agency from some random Internet link. The perks of Hollywood royalty never end. And don't worry, I followed the rules and haven't told *anyone* about it. Can I tell you how fun it is to have a secret like this when basically my whole life is documented?

This couldn't have come at a more perfect time, because I am in desperate need of a vacation from my mom, Gina Chase. Yes, THE Gina Chase—heiress to the Davidson carpet fortune and an Academy Award–winning legend of the big screen. You've seen her in *Unspooled Love, Surrender a Moment, Once Upon an Island, The Alligator Club*; and she hates when I mention this, but she also was on an awful cop show for three episodes. She recently divorced her second husband, Internet mogul Mason Gravis.

She is also trying to ruin my life.

She wants us to take this mommy-daughter trip to Tharma. She did a movie there back in the nineties, and feels like going back will be some spiritual awakening. So she got a yacht and wants me to experience the culture with her. Culture. Um, no thanks. The only thing I want to experience on vacation is some tanning oil and a bunch of magazines. And with my new fragrance line and the MTV hosting gig and all the time I've spent in the studio, I really need a relaxing vacation.

Of course, Mom would be seriously upset if she found out I skipped out on our whole bonding thing. I know she's got big plans for us—I shudder to think what they are. All you have to do is go along with her craziness, but don't get too excited. You still have to be me, right? And for the love of all that is holy, no embarrassing paparazzi moments once you're off the boat. I have a relatively clean record and would like to keep it that way.

Speaking of paparazzi, I take a lot of pride that I have yet to make a worst-dressed list. I design my own clothes and live for fashion, plus I have my personal stylist/designer, Ryder, to help me. He's so fab and sooooo expensive. Actually, looking like me is always expensive, so please keep up my beauty routine. I'll be livid if I come back to ragged cuticles, K? Oh AND I'm on this special diet and exercise plan called Wheels, No Meals. I roller-skate when I'm not wearing heels, and don't eat too much. I've already lost two pounds!

Last thing: make sure you talk and text Barrett a bit. A BIT. I hate it when girls try to creep on my man. So communicate only enough that he doesn't suspect I'm gone. Which should be easy since he's supposed to be halfway around the world on a fishing trip with his little brother.

Remember. Mom = Bond. And be careful not to let her talk you into doing anything I wouldn't do.

"Floressa Chase? I'm confused. I thought Façade only deals with legitimate royals. I mean, besides the watcher and trial gigs. What makes Hollywood royalty Level Two?"

"I can't fully answer that. Suffice it to say Floressa's connections go beyond her mother. To test our findings, we put out what we call a feeler ad online—only someone with some trace of regal blood would see it, not that she knows that."

"Still, everyone has a great-great-great dead royal in

their family somewhere," I reasoned. "What makes Floressa special enough for a sub?"

"It's not just royal connections, although that certainly is the main criterion. Part of what qualifies a client for a higher level is wealth and exposure. Floressa has those coming out of her heiress ears."

"So all I have to do is hang out with a super-famous actress on a yacht next to some exotic island."

"Yes. I'm glad it seems simple to you. Keep it that way. Since I'm taking personal time while you're on this job, I may be difficult to contact if you need me. But you won't need me."

I hardly heard her. All my pre-play anxiety melted away, replaced with complete rapture. In my wildest dreams, I'd never imagined an opportunity like this. "I get to be Floressa Chase! I get to be Floressa Chase!"

"Calm down. Floressa Chase does not squeal." Meredith sighed. "I'm dropping you off in the yacht bathroom, so it's a tight fit. You dock in Tharma in two days. And watch out for the spicy food. I may be dropping you off in a bathroom, but there is no reason for you to spend your entire sub job there."

I'd woken up this morning, nervous about acting, with no clue that I was about to play a much bigger role. A *red carpet* role. This far exceeded my princess dreams.

I hopped out of the bubble, nearly stepping into the bathroom wall. "Oof," I said, turning around to see a mirror. I swallowed another squeal. There I was, starring as Floressa Chase in a green striped bikini, dark shades resting on my head. I flipped her black hair and smiled over my shoulder. There were thousands of girls who would love to be Floressa Chase. I was the only one, besides her, who actually was.

A tightness clamped my ankles, and my feet grew heavy. The yacht swayed, sending me reeling—no, make that *wheeling*—into the counter. Oh, great. I knew Floressa was doing the roller-skating diet, but on a boat? How did she stop herself from rolling overboard?

I opened the door and edged along the walls until I reached the stairs. Placing the toe of the skate along each step, I bumped my way up. I let out a sigh when I reached the top, holding out my arms to ensure my balance as I faced the top deck.

The sun bounced off the crystal blue water. I could barely see the outline of land in the far distance. The salty air was ribboned with a light breeze, perfect for lounging. Which was exactly what Gina Chase was doing in one of the many padded deck chairs.

It's generally known that celebrities are airbrushed and made up in photographs and movies, and that in real life they have zits, bad hair, and cellulite like everyone else. Maybe that's true for other celebrities, but Gina Chase's appearance verged on perfect. One look and you knew she was *someone*. She had the same dark hair and vibrant smile as Floressa, but her cheetah-print, one-piece suit complemented her creamy skin and sultry curves. I could almost place her in the same exalted category as my favorite fifties and sixties icons. Almost.

She tugged off her sunglasses. "Flossie! Where have you been? Don't answer—I'm sure it involves those silly roller skates. Tell me, what do you want Johann to make for lunch?"

I considered my first question. Millie had been so exact on these sort of details, but I didn't need everything outlined to make an educated guess. I'd survived on practically zero information as a Level One, and it's not like Floressa was this big enigma. So rich girl on the ocean would want . . . "Uh, lobster sounds yummy."

Gina chuckled "Since when do you eat lobster, or anything over a hundred calories?"

"Ha. Just kidding." Oh, yeah. Rich girl on ocean doing the Wheels, No Meals diet. I prayed her meal plan didn't involve counting calories and carbs—I had no clue how that worked. Lobster is a fish—isn't that good for you? "I'll have . . . a salad?"

"Let's indulge and add some grilled chicken to it. Johann?"

All the yacht catalogues I'd flipped through had a dimpled, chiseled Johann, whose side job was likely modeling for Ralph Lauren ads. He wouldn't even need to change his polo shirt. When he left to get our food, I rolled at slow-motion speed until I made it to the chair next to Gina.

She rubbed my arm. "Are you all right? You seem wobbly."

"Hungry. That salad should be yum." I untied my laces, removed the skates, and stuffed them into Floressa's bag. "Don't want tan lines."

Gina went back to the script she was reading. I tried hard not to stare. Although I'd met countless royals during my adventures, it was still different from seeing an actress—an actress who was in movies and magazines and hair dye commercials. Part of me wanted to reach out and touch her cheekbones to check that she was really real.

"So you've gone thirty entire seconds without complaining about being on this yacht. Are you finally having a change of heart?"

"No." I said, remembering this job's balancing act: bond with mom and act like I was barely tolerating it. "I think the rocking of this boat is wearing me down."

"Yachts don't rock. It's that ridiculous roller-skating diet. Why don't you do some yoga with me instead? Wonderful boost to your immune system, and you're going to need your energy when we land. I have some surprises for you."

I could only imagine what kind of surprises Gina would shower upon her daughter. I tried to act bored. "I'm sure it'll be just as exciting as the rest of the trip."

"I want this to be a spiritual awakening for you. When was the last time you connected to your inner child?"

"Um, never?"

"Exactly. That's why I've divided the next two days into three categories. Mind, body, and soul. Although we may switch up the order—do mind today, soul tomorrow, and end with body. We have a congratulatory pamper session booked. Doing this together will draw us closer as a family, and we'll need that foundation when we arrive in Tharma."

"Why? What happens in Tharma?"

Gina opened her mouth like she was going to say more, then closed it slowly. "Mind, body, and soul first, Flossie. Now, go into the study and find an enriching book. No pink covers! We want depth!"

The next two days were so deep, I felt like I was drowning. Drowning in AWESOME. I was making money doing activities most people would pay a fortune for. I didn't know if I had any "inner child" action going on, but my one-on-one time with Gina Chase was golden.

On the first day, we talked about politics and books and Gina's religious awakenings. And when I started asking her questions about her theater background, she poured out information, revealing how she tapped into her emotions, how she kept a straight face when things were funny, tips for line memorization. I think she was flattered that her daughter was finally interested, when in reality, she was being grilled by a small-town theater newbie.

The second day—our communion with our souls— was devoted to lots of self-exploration and discussion. We explored why Floressa preferred the color purple to green. Gina talked about her childhood fear of puppies. And we ended the day on the deck, meditating as the sun set.

It was during my quiet meditation time that the initial *I am Floressa Chase* shock wore off, and I started to consider what I wanted to accomplish while on this job. I was so busy going fangirl on Gina, I hadn't thought about MP. And except for my transformation (which was the work of the Rouge), I hadn't felt the buzzing once. If I ever wanted to discover more about magic's possibility, or figure out Façade secrets, I would need to stay focused, Academy Award–winning actress or not.

On the third day, I awoke to a man in blue suede pants flicking cold water on me. Gina had neglected to include aquatic attack in the schedule.

"What?" I sat up and covered my face with my arms. "What do you want?"

The man set the glass of water on my small bedside table and gestured to my hair. "Would you look at this? I have less than three hours to get you photo friendly."

I squinted at him, finally remembering Floressa's profile. "You're the stylist. Ryder."

"Honey, don't play the ditz with me. Too much to do."

I flipped off the covers and slid out of bed. "Hold on. Bathroom." I paused at the door. "Nice pants."

"My personal fashion theme this week is Elvis. Naturally, blue suede shoes are too predictable."

I brushed my teeth and splashed water on my face. Ryder was placing a mint on my pillow when I opened the door. The rest of the room had been tidied, and smelled fresh.

Ryder started talking without looking up. "Couldn't help myself. The aura of this place was stagnant. So." He turned to face me. "Big news flash: As soon as we docked this morning, a call came in from the palace. The king has invited you and your mother to dinner. THE. KING. I think he's hoping your mom is going to do another movie here." Ryder cocked an eyebrow up at me, but I had no clue how to interpret it. "Of course, your mother is in an absolute tizzy, so as soon as I'm done with you, I'll have to talk her down. Gina Chase does not play the tizzy role well."

"She's met royalty before. Barrett's royalty." I sat down on the bed. "Maybe she's surprised by the invite."

"Whatever. If her skin breaks out, I'll have to dig in to my antistress remedies. Again. So I already drew your baths for you on the deck. First mud, then my own special blend of rose petals and mint infusion. Then there's your mani and pedi of course—your cuticles must be weeping after a week of going unattended—and don't hate me, but Gloria had an award show *emergency* so I had to get another aesthetician flown in stat. I have your wardrobe choices prepared in the leisure area, although now with this extra engagement, I hope fifteen outfits is enough of a choice. Oh! And I know there was much debate on this, but did you decide on curls or casual chignon? Personally, with this humidity, I think you're safer with the curls. More carefree and innocent. Remember, your image consultant recommends you not deviate far from the girl-next-door model. I've also ordered you a fruit plate for breakfast. Easy on the cantaloupe."

Ryder walked out the door, leaving me sitting on the bed, openmouthed. Was that English he was speaking? Or Hollywood?

"Let's go!" he called. "And leave those tacky roller skates under your bed."

I scrambled out of my cabin and into a day filled with beauty horrors too graphic to replay. By that afternoon, I'd been nipped, trimmed, tucked, coifed, and rolled into an emerald green sundress with stilettos so high they made the roller skates seem practical. I teetered on the deck, my stomach rumbling and my feet already hurting. Focusing on mind and soul was far more doable than this.

"You would swear you've never worn five-inch heels before. Poise! Poise!" Ryder said.

"Not on a swaying yacht," I whined, not caring if I was in or out of character at this point.

"There's my precious daughter." Gina glided across the deck, not an ounce of worry or stress evident on her face. I hadn't seen her much that day, what with our different beauty teams working their torture. "Sorry if Ryder was rough on you, but you'll thank me when you see what your surprise is. Or, rather, who."

"Ryder already told me about the king."

"Not a king, but you're not far off."

"Floressa? Babe, get down here!" someone called from the dock. I hobbled to the edge of the yacht and looked down to see Prince Barrett beaming up at me. "Surprised?"

My mouth hung open. Surprised? Um, yeah. I'd written two texts to him during the last couple of days and thought my Barrett business was done. Now the arrogant, gorgeous prince who I wasn't even supposed to talk to, let alone *see*, was only a few feet away. I turned to Gina. "That's my surprise?"

She clapped her hands together. "You get so little vacation time. And you were such a sport about this trip, I thought you deserved some paparazzi-free time with your boyfriend. I love that you had no clue! Did you like his fishing trip lie? Barrett flew in with his brother—"

"His brother?" The words scratched my throat.

"Yes, well, you know how his parents are about Barrett's need for a chaperone. Don't worry, Prince Karl won't be hanging around the whole time."

"Prince Karl is *here?* On the island? *This* island?"

"Yes." Gina rolled her eyes. "And so is your boyfriend. Really, Flossie, this isn't difficult to comprehend. Now run down there and have a moment before we leave for dinner."

Ryder fluffed my hair. "Please promise you'll be mindful of your lip gloss situation. I'll be on call if there are any emergencies."

Lip gloss emergencies? PRINCE KARL WAS ON THE ISLAND. Lip gloss was the least of my worries.

Chapter 17

I hobbled over to the dock entrance, taking careful steps down the ramp and onto dry land. Walking is usually a skill that comes easily to me. I have been doing it since I was one. But there was the whole roller-skating/stiletto/sea-legs dilemma. Even worse, Karl picked that precise moment to step out of the limo and join his brother.

And then, I forgot everything. Walking. Legs. Those things you put your shoes on that are attached to legs. Oh, right. Feet. Who could worry about the details when the boy I'd been dreaming about for months was right there in front of me? I could just . . . reach out and touch him.

He smiled politely when I approached. My legs wobbled

from the smile and I lurched forward. Karl caught me. "Are you all right?"

I don't know how many times I'd fantasized about being in Karl's arms. How we would connect, and no matter who I was in that moment, he would know I was ME and that I was the one he loved. But Karl was stiff with his embrace, making the contact far less epic than I'd hoped. The truth was, I wasn't me. I was Floressa, Karl's brother's girlfriend. Floressa and Karl had probably never touched beyond a handshake. I tried to right myself again, but my legs were still two sticks of Jell-O. Barrett finally grasped my hand and wrapped me in his arms.

"Lay off my goods, brude."

"I was helping her." Karl's face went red. "Please forgive the familiarity, Floressa."

"Maybe you should learn to hold on to your own girl instead," Barrett said.

"That wasn't necessary." Karl was so cute when he was uncomfortable! "I was only helping."

"I'm kidding." Barrett gazed down at me. "Now, *you* look delicious."

I pinched a smile onto my face. Being flopped from one prince to another was beyond disorienting. "Thanks."

"And you're so adorable when you pretend to be embarrassed. As if you don't know that you're the most gorgeous girl on this island." He squeezed me tighter. "I'm so glad we're going to be together tonight."

"Together?" I asked. "But Gina and I are meeting with the king."

"I'm in on the invite. It's not every day the Crown Prince of Fenmar rolls up to town. And I'm hoping your mom distracts the king so we can be alone."

In the last five minutes I'd gone from text messaging to finding myself in Barrett's embrace. And although he was hot (*very, very hot*), this wasn't what I wanted or needed right now. I still had to wrap my head around the fact that Karl was here and . . . Floressa was going to freak. "Alone? Well, what is Karl doing?"

Barrett turned to his brother. "Karl will probably spend the night listening to Celine Dion, eating ice cream, and crying manly tears."

"Why?"

"Ress, you should have seen it. He had a major falling-out with Olivia. And by falling-out, I mean she was throwing china at him while he sat there making his I-must-be-a-proper-prince face. Entertaining, but pathetic."

"Hold on. It wasn't like that." Karl shuffled his foot on the deck. "We're amicable. Olivia was simply heated in the moment."

"Heated when she saw that tabloid picture. It's so wonderfully sordid, isn't it? Finally I'm not the prince on the cover. Finally Mum and Dad are giving lectures to Karl on proper behavior."

"So, are you broken up?" I asked Karl, trying to keep the hope out of my voice.

"For now." Karl ran a hand down his face. "Rather, we're . . . taking a break. It's not as dramatic as Barrett is painting it."

"They're done," Barrett said. "Which is too bad because Olivia may have been crazy, but she was hot. Not as hot as you, though, babe."

"I'd appreciate it if you don't talk about Olivia that way."

"Although, so is that Elsa chick. She's got that whole farm-girl thing going for her."

Karl cut Barrett an angry look. "Leave Elsa out of this, too. Truly, Barrett, you're worse than the press."

"I'm proud of you, brude. I was starting to wonder if you were human."

Karl and Olivia broke up. If they broke up, then Karl was single. His brother mentioned the Elsa tabloid. Had he talked to Elsa? What would happen now?

Forget that. What about *right now*? Karl was standing directly in front of me. He would be alone tonight. Eating ice cream. Crying manly tears and . . . Oh, please, let the Celine Dion part be a joke.

"You should come with us," I said, my words tumbling out before I could even consider them. Hey, it wasn't entirely self-serving. Having another person around would be a great barrier between Barrett and me. "It is a royal thing and you *are* royal. Plus, no one should be alone right after a breakup."

"Well"—Karl glanced at Barrett—"it *would* be nice to get out after being cooped up on that plane."

Barrett squeezed my waist and lowered his voice. "But what about our alone time, babe?"

"Later! I'm still . . . seasick anyway."

"You're on land now."

"Landsick then. Or I have sea legs." I moved his hand off my waist. "We'll have gallons of time together tomorrow. Gina won't mind. Tonight, I'm lucky to have two royal escorts."

Barrett tapped me on my nose. "You always want more, don't you?"

I glanced back and forth between the two princes. *If by more, you mean more drama, then yes. Apparently I do.*

The palace was amazing. Of course. It's a palace. What else would it be? But I was so nervous about having Karl appear out of nowhere, not to mention eating with my famous actress mother, my hot prince boyfriend, and some random king, that I barely took in anything. Oh, fancy chandelier. Line of servants. Expensive art and lots of breakable stuff, like a life-size bronze elephant statue in the entryway.

I didn't have to worry about deflecting Barrett too much, because Gina insisted on holding my hand. She startled at every noise and her skin was cold and clammy. I found it oddly comforting that someone as famous as Gina would be nervous.

I wondered how big this night would be for Floressa. She'd had no clue her boyfriend was going to show up. Maybe she'd rather be on the island after all. At the very least, I could tell her about the changes in the schedule.

Surely Façade would approve of contact if it was in the client's best interest.

I could find a way to talk to her. Floressa was all over the Internet.

I asked a servant to show me the bathroom before we met with the king. The pamper room—with a sitting area and four sinks—wasn't as private as I'd hoped, so I sat down on the toilet and wrote a text to Meredith.

> **Desi:** Barrett showed up as a surprise for Floressa AND
> we're dining with the King of Tharma. Think Floressa might
> want to know. Can you make that happen?

I sat and stared at the screen for the next five minutes. Meredith had never taken this long to reply. I wrote another one:

> **Desi:** URGENT!!!! ASAP!!! 911!! MEREDITH?

Another five minutes of "radio silence." I couldn't keep everyone waiting much longer. I scrolled back to Floressa's page. No contact and no chat room information because she was a new client. Desperate, I Googled her name and found a social-networking account. She got hundreds of messages a day, and she probably wasn't checking, but what else could I do?

> Floressa,
> I've been "skating" around things all day, but now I'm in

"royal" trouble and can use your help before the "sub" sinks. Please contact me at audreyfan@facademail.com for further details. Not looking for money. Just want to help.

D

Our dinner party was small, even if the dinner *table* was not. Barrett sat to my left, with Karl and Gina across from us. We all stood when a servant announced the royal family's entry.

The doors swung open, revealing King Aung and a nine- or ten-year-old girl with wispy bangs and small features. She rushed over to the seat on my right.

"Wow. Floressa Chase! I feel like I know you already."

"Oh. Well, thank you . . . Princess."

"Princess Isla. I want to be just like you. Where did you get that dress?"

I looked down at it, kicking myself for not checking the designer. "Um, from my closet."

"Oh my gosh! Did you hear that, father? She's funny. Floressa Chase told me a joke."

"You must excuse my daughter's enthusiasm." King Aung smiled. "It's an exciting dinner crowd, even for us. Please have a seat."

"I bet you designed it yourself," Isla chattered on as we all sat. "Did you design it yourself? I have everything from your spring season. Magenta is so hot right now, isn't it?"

"Magenta? Uh, yes. Blazing."

King Aung chuckled. There was something startlingly

familiar about him, but I couldn't figure out what it was. Well, he was a *king*, and handsome. For an old guy. I'd probably noticed his picture in the manual.

I watched each of the party guests, trying to gauge what they knew about each other based on their mannerisms and expressions. Gina seemed to agree about the handsome part—she didn't take her eyes off the king once.

"I appreciate your accepting our invitation, Miss Chase."

"Are you seriously going to use 'Miss' on me? Come on, Aung. It's Gina."

We all stiffened at Gina's use of the king's first name. He smiled graciously. "Of course, Gina. Old friends can be more . . . familiar, I suppose."

Barrett cocked an eyebrow at me. Old friends?

Gina's laugh tinkled, but there was something hysterical underneath it. "Yes, it's been a while since I filmed *Once Upon an Island*. It's a tragedy it's taken me so long to return. I'd say about seventeen years."

The king took a sip of water. "Remarkable. Time flies, does it not?"

"In some ways, yes. In others, no."

They exchanged a meaningful glance. Barrett kicked me under the table and mouthed "What's going on?" I shook my head. How would I know how Gina knew the king? She hadn't mentioned any connection when we'd discussed the invite.

"Yes, *Once Upon an Island* was a joy to work on, especially since I took time off after to have Floressa."

"This I know," King Aung said. "And now, here she is."

"Oh, sorry." Gina beamed at me. "I forgot introductions."

She introduced me, and I smiled despite the king's somber gaze. Barrett and Karl knew the king from royal circles, and together eased into a conversation about their favorite golf heroes. The first course was brought out. Gina continued to gawk at the king, so I turned to Isla.

"I like your necklace."

She grasped the chain. "You wore one like it to the *Rose and Water* premier. That was when you were dating Charles Voorhees, who I'm sure is nice, but he is no Prince Barrett. Don't you agree?"

"You remember what necklace I wore?"

"I told you, I am your biggest fan. I'm actually in your fan club, but I used a false name to hide my identity. You don't know what it's like to meet you. You're my idol!"

I played with my napkin. "Thanks."

"I can't tell you how excited I was when my dad said you were coming over. I mean, I knew he'd met your mom, because he has a picture of them together in his office—"

"He does?"

"It was taken when she did that movie. I used to play with it when I was younger, pretend like Gina was my aunt and we were cousins. I've been begging to meet you for months. Usually, father agrees right away—I've met many celebrities. But you, he always brushed away. Then when your mom's manager called and said she was coming to visit . . . well, it was perfect. I asked my father to have a dinner as an early birthday present to me."

"It's your birthday?"

"In five months." She grabbed my arm. "Do you want to see my closet? The palace?"

I snuck another glance at Gina, who was sneaking a glance at the king, who was sneaking a glance back at her. "Actually, why don't you show me your dad's office and that picture of my mom?"

Chapter
18

When dinner was over, Isla took us around the palace while the king showed Gina the outside gardens. I let Barrett hold my hand (um, yeah—held a royal heartthrob's hand, another job duty) as Isla gabbed on about room after room, and Karl trailed behind us.

Barrett whispered in my ear. "Let's ditch the third and fourth wheel and go explore on our own."

"We can't. Isla's too excited."

"I wish we were the ones touring the garden, not your mom and King Aung."

I glanced back at Karl, who looked so cute and troubled. Was he thinking of Olivia or Elsa with that far-off expression? He caught me staring and covered up his anguish with a polite smile. I turned around. Last time I'd toured a garden, it had been with him. The garden tour, actually, was when I'd started to like Karl. What my mom said when we saw his magazine picture was true—Karl wasn't drop-dead gorgeous like Barrett. But, for that one clear day in the Alps, he'd let his walls down, and I'd seen a guy who was funny, smart, and sweet. That's what mattered.

Nope. Don't go there. Right now I had the other garden tour to consider. Why did Gina and the king go off together? It couldn't be proper. I mean, they were both single—the king widowed and Gina twice divorced—but this could lead to rumors, and Gina was usually so aware of her image. Then again, it could be a friendly stroll. They obviously knew each other. Maybe they just wanted to catch up.

We came to the study, crammed with towering book-shelves and a jungle of exotic plants. One table displayed photos of the king and the many political and entertainment figures he'd met.

"There's your mom." Isla pointed to a framed 5 x 7 print right in the middle. "She's pretty there, but I think she's prettier now."

"They look *friendly*," Barrett said.

I peered closer. I'd seen *Once Upon an Island*—in the photo Gina wore the dark blue Victorian-era dress from the movie's famous ship-departure scene. The king's white shirt was untucked and unbuttoned, his arm draped over Gina's shoulders. She leaned into him as he looked down at her, grinning. Not the pose of casual acquaintances.

The autograph from Gina read "To My Love."

My stomach lurched as the details clicked into place. Gina's nerves about seeing the king. Her hints to Floressa about impeding big news. Their unescorted stroll through the garden, the informality, the secret looks, the photo, the inscription . . .

Floressa's age.

No wonder the king looked so familiar. If you took those two beautiful people and mixed them together, you would have Floressa.

My voice caught in my throat. I looked wildly at Barrett, but he was busy analyzing a picture of Bruce Willis. Karl, however, caught my eye and whispered, "Are you all right?"

All right? ALL RIGHT? No, Karl. So. Not. All right. "This room is stuffy," I said to Isla. "Can you show me another?"

"Sure. I can show you my closet!" Isla squealed. "I'll put on a green dress, and it'll be like we're sisters."

I swallowed. Sisters. You don't know the half of it, girl.

Karl and Barrett opted to play pool in the game room while Isla showed off her wardrobe. It took ten outfit changes before I could form a course of action. All I had to do was ditch Isla and go find Gina and ask her the scoop— Was the king Floressa's father?

While Isla changed, I buried myself behind a rack of dresses and thumbed through my manual for information on the king. My quick research revealed that King Aung had been married fourteen years ago and lost his wife to cancer when Isla was five. Originally the second brother in line to the crown, Aung's older brother was assassinated during a time of political unrest, leaving the kingdom to Aung. This happened while the filming of *Once Upon an Island* was ending, and the crew quickly left because of the ensuing riots. Some of the last movie shots had to be filmed in California.

Aung was Floressa's dad. Forget spiritual awakening; this was a big bomb, and Floressa had no clue it was about to go off. If I thought Barrett's arrival was a reason to contact her, discovering a secret royal father was an emergency.

Meredith's phone went right to voice mail, so I shot her another 911 text and checked my e-mail. Nothing from Floressa. Without a means to contact her, there was little I could do until I heard from Meredith. Best to gather more information. I needed to verify this discovery.

"Do you think this dress looks better in gray or plum?"

I shoved my manual into my purse and turned around. Isla held two identical-except-for-color dresses against her.

"Plum." I stood. "Although the gray is pretty too. You should put it on. I'm going to go find the princes. Why don't you meet us in the game room?"

"Can you find the game room on your own? People are always getting lost in the palace."

"Oh, yeah. I have, like, a built-in navigational system in my brain."

Isla opened her mouth wide. "That is so cool."

I hurried out of the closet. I did have a navigational

system, but it was in my manual, and I needed it to guide me to the gardens. I didn't have much time before Isla and the boys started to wonder where I was.

I heard Gina's and King Aung's voices after I crossed the sprawling lawn. The moon was full and the sky clear, which helped me see my way as I tiptoed behind the hedge of bushes circling the courtyard and fountains. The king and Gina sat on a bench with two bodyguards a respectful distance away. I crouched behind a bush close enough to hear, but far enough that *they* couldn't hear *me*.

"Spielberg is a gem to work with," Gina was saying. "Other directors lose their artistic edge when they reach that level."

"Gina, enough of the preliminaries. Will you please explain why you decided to return to my country after all these years?"

Gina broke a leaf off a bush and twirled it in her hands. "Floressa and I aren't as close as we used to be. I thought it'd be nice to bond with her, to help her connect to her spiritual side. I have such fond memories of the time I spent here before—"

"You didn't tell her about *us*, did you?"

"And what if I had?" Gina sat up straighter. "Would you have been ashamed?"

"Of course not. But you know no good can come from our past being exposed." The king glanced at his security guards and lowered his voice. "Our life together—it was an enjoyable time."

"*Enjoyable time*? Aung, I loved you."

"Did you? Because, as I recall, you left me when I was already at rock bottom. The only thing that comforted me when my brother was assassinated was knowing that you would be my queen."

"But I'm not a queen! I couldn't even play that role in a movie. And you weren't the next in line when we eloped. I married the second prince, not a king. When your brother died, that changed everything. We couldn't move to California. You had a duty to your country."

"And to you! I would have done anything for you. But, instead, I found out from a *tabloid* that you were dating that producer." The king folded his arms across his broad chest. "I'm just glad I annulled our marriage here, otherwise I don't believe your next quick wedding would have been legitimate. The ring I gave you . . . I wonder . . . Did you take it off before you put the other one on?"

Gina shoved her right hand in front of the king's face. "I still wear it. I've worn it every day for seventeen years. You and I both know it was a promise you couldn't keep, not with your title. I left because I loved you, Aung, and I knew I wasn't best for you. But don't you for a second think my feelings weren't real."

"Your actions don't match your words, my dear." Aung hung his head in his hands. "Let's not open this wound any more. We were young and we've moved on. What's past is past."

Gina glanced up at the bodyguards. "It's not that easy."

"It is. I am king now. A scandal for me is a scandal for

my country. And I have quite a bit more pride than to accept your belated advances."

"That's not why I'm here." Gina drew in a breath, preparing herself for the delivery of her greatest line yet. "After I left you, I returned to L.A. and married Lorenzo because I didn't want scandal either. I knew what that would mean to you *and* your country."

"We could have worked through it. We could have gotten married again, given my people something to be excited about. Yes, you aren't royal, but—"

"That's not the scandal I'm talking about." She glanced over to the bushes, and I crouched lower. "Haven't you ever done the math with Floressa's age? And look at her—Lorenzo had red hair and freckles. Did you notice that she has your eyes and coloring and . . . your laugh? She's . . . she's yours."

A mixture of emotions flashed across the king's face. Confusion, understanding, fear, anger. But none of them joy. His voice was tense when he spoke. "It cannot be."

I closed my eyes for a moment and prayed the king would be sympathetic. Yes, finding out you have a teenage daughter with the-girl-that-ran-away isn't your average after-dinner chat. And no matter her reasons, Gina shouldn't have kept this from him. Gina shouldn't have done a lot of things. But now that he knew, he could be the better person. I'd seen how he looked at Isla with adoration. Floressa deserved that too. She was innocent in this. Even if they kept it a secret from the press, King Aung could still be a piece of Floressa's private world.

When I opened my eyes, the king was standing. He pointed at Gina. "I want you to listen carefully. You will not share this news with anyone. If you do, I shall deny it. You will not sail into my country and ruin everything. You are an *actress*." He spit the last word out. "I will not have you disgracing me."

"Aung, please. I know I don't deserve your love. I ran away from it. But Floressa had no part in this. She doesn't even know. I was hoping—"

"Enough!" King Aung boomed. "I will have my own people confirm this news." He shot a look at his bodyguards. "This meeting did not take place. I hope you understand if I return to formalities, Miss Chase. You may see your way out."

The king stormed out of the courtyard. A breeze picked up. I wrapped my arms around myself, waiting for Gina to leave. She started crying, and I felt awful that I couldn't slip away and give her the privacy she deserved.

Gina's sobs quieted. "You can come out now, Flossie. I know you're behind that bush."

So much for sneaking away. I stood, slowly, so that I was level with the hedge. "What just happened?"

"Come sit next to me."

I circled the hedge until I came to an opening and slid next to Gina on the bench. Her face was already puffy, and she had snot running down her nose. Still, she looked beautiful. Vulnerable, sad, and beautiful. "That's not how I wanted you to hear the news," she said.

Floressa would probably huff off at this moment. And

she'd be justified in that. But I couldn't bring myself to do it. I felt so bad for Gina, for Floressa. I sat there and let Gina cry, keeping my face blank.

"So this is why you brought me here," I said.

Gina blew her nose. "I was going to tell you before we got off the yacht, but then I worried you wouldn't come and then never meet him. You have to understand his reaction had nothing to do with you. It would be shocking news under any circumstance."

"Why didn't you tell him before?" I asked.

"I don't know. No, I do. I was trying to protect you." She crumpled up her tissue. "Aung and I married in secret because we thought it was romantic—we planned to tell his family right before moving to California to start a new life. Then his brother was killed and Aung had to stay. I found out I was pregnant, and for the first time, I was scared. After all the political chaos, the last thing this country needed was me. And the last thing you needed was to grow up both a princess and Gina Chase's daughter. But Aung wouldn't have accepted that. Things are more black and white to him."

There was some logic to Gina's reasoning. *Some.* But I couldn't say that. This was something Floressa needed to hear and digest on her own, without me putting words in her mouth. What I wouldn't do to beam her back right now, to let her feel this moment herself. I squeezed Gina's hand. "I don't know what to think right now. I need some time."

"Of course. I think Aung, your father, needs the same thing."

I let go of her hand. "Then let's not talk about this again until I'm ready."

"Don't you have questions—"

"Later. I'm going to find Barrett and Karl. I think our welcome has worn itself out."

I hurried across the lawn. Now, this, THIS would be a time when knowing exactly how my magic worked would be great. Magical power, or even a sixth sense, could get me connected to Floressa, whether emotionally or in person. Sure, princesses don't want their vacations ruined, but this was the biggest drama I had ever encountered. No amount of BEST research or client background checks could replace knowing exactly what Floressa wanted me to do.

This was a scandal. A major tabloid-crushing, life-ruining royal scandal that I did not want to mess up.

I slowed my steps, a memory sparking to life. When I very first became a sub, I overheard Meredith talking to Floressa Chase on the phone. Confused, I'd asked about Floressa's agency eligibility, but Meredith had said something . . . something about Floressa's "status" changing. Oh, and that Façade knew things the tabloids didn't.

So the agency *did* know Floressa was a princess. And of course she was. Façade was so strict about magic, they wouldn't waste it in a non-royal. I should have known there was more going on. Wasn't there some sort of moral obligation to tell Floressa the truth? Just like there had to be a moral obligation to tell those poor sub hopefuls about sub sanitization?

No. I could worry about Façade's involvement later. That was a sparkly can of glittery worms I didn't have time to open right now. The most important thing was to get a hold of Floressa.

I'd just reached the sprawling palace terrace when my manual buzzed. Finally. I glanced around to check that I was still alone in the darkness. I thought for sure it was Meredith informing me she was on her way. After all, she'd intervened when I kissed Karl. If a kiss was an emergency, what category did a secret celebrity princess fall under?

Not Meredith. Better. Floressa.

Floressa: I got your message. Who are you? What do you know?

I texted back.

Me: Sorry. I'm your sub. I couldn't get in contact with you any other way.
Floressa: Oh. What do you want? I'm supposed to be relaxing over here.

Uh, where did I start? Remember how you said to leave your boyfriend alone? Well, he's here. Oh, and your mother's ex-husband is a king—and guess what?—he's your dad and Isla is your half sister and you are a princess.

Also, your roller skates give me blisters.

Me: I don't think it's something I can tell you in a text. Lots of stuff is going on here. You should get back.

Floressa: But I've paid for two more days.

Me: I'm sure you can get a refund.

Floressa: Just tell me.

Before I could text back, a shadow fell on the terrace. I quickly hid the manual.

"Barrett sent me to look for you," Karl said. "He wants to leave soon."

I faked a smile. "Of course. I just wanted a moment. It's a beautiful night."

"My word, that breeze is unseasonably cool. Take my coat." Karl slipped off his suit jacket and slid it over my shoulders. It smelled like him—like expensive cars and mint. He sat in the chair next to me, a respectful distance away.

"You can hear the ocean from here. Does it sound the same in California?"

"Same ocean." I pulled Karl's coat tighter around me, overcome with the sudden urge to cry. I couldn't control King Aung's feelings. I couldn't take the hurt away for Gina or Floressa. What *use* was I here? I had actual magical abilities, but I was being used as a puppet stand-in. I wasn't special. I could have been anyone.

And then I did cry. Not loud. Silent tears.

"Shall we go find Barrett—" Karl noticed my tears

and stopped. "Oh. Forgive me. Did I say something to upset you?"

I shook my head.

"Would you like to talk about it?"

More than anything I wanted to talk about it. No, I wanted to get out of here, back home to my calm, scandal-free Idaho life. "I'm fine. Let me . . . let me gain my composure. I don't want Barrett to see me like this."

"Maybe Barrett *should* see you like this. He can console you far better than I can. Unless he's the reason you're upset, in which case I'll take care of him."

"How?"

"A duel. We're royal." Karl cracked a rare smile. "It's allowed."

My laugh turned into a hiccup. "It's not Barrett. Barrett's great. There's . . . there's been a lot of change in my life lately, and I have some hard choices to make. I'm trying to get through it."

"Can I offer a bit of advice, then?" Karl tapped his chest. "Think with this. My brain led me astray for far too long, and I'm much happier now that I've followed my heart."

I couldn't help myself. I had to bring it up. "Is that what you did with Elsa?"

Karl blushed. "Ah, that's a topic for another time. Let's not worry about my troubles now." He stood. "But as far as your troubles go, if you ever want to talk, I'm here. We're nearly family, after all."

I stumbled up and wiped at my tears. My head was telling

me to jump ship, but my heart knew I had to help Floressa as best I could. "Thanks, Karl. You really are a prince."

"Speaking of, let's get you to my brother." He held out his arm and I took it, trying my best to ignore the tingles that it brought.

Barrett and Isla were waiting for us in the sitting room. Barrett hugged me when I came in. "There you are. I thought you'd been kidnapped. Why are you wearing Karl's coat?"

I snuck one more sniff before taking the coat off and handing it to Karl. "I was cold. Have you seen my mom?"

"She's waiting in the limo. Did you make her mad again? I passed her in the hallway and she barreled right past me."

"She looked like she was crying," Isla added.

A servant clicked his heels in the doorway. "His Majesty has fallen ill and has retired for the evening. He apologizes, but bids you a warm farewell."

Isla rolled her eyes. "My dad gets antisocial sometimes. Promise me we can meet again. How long are you here?"

"Um, I don't know."

"I'll talk to Dad. We will set up something."

I'm sure he's looking at his calendar right now, little sis.

Chapter
19

I faked a headache when we got back to the yacht, promising Barrett we'd go sightseeing the next day. I only hoped Floressa, the real Floressa, would be back by then.

I clicked back to my text message conversation with Floressa and stared at the screen. **Just tell me.** Should I? I had a suspicion I was breaking rules here, but I had to get her back home.

> **Desi:** Hey, it's me again. Your sub.
> **Floressa:** Oh my gosh, first you desert me and now you're interrupting my beauty rest. Different time zone, ever heard of it? What do you want?
> **Desi:** Well, first off, Barrett is here.

Floressa: What? Barrett is THERE? What he is doing there?

Desi: Your mom brought him as a surprise. Well, as moral support.

Floressa: Moral support for what? You aren't kissing him, are you? ARE YOU?

Oh, honey. If only that was your biggest problem.

Desi: No. She probably brought him because she had big news. About your dad.

Floressa: Lorenzo? I haven't seen Lorenzo in ten years. What is my mom doing talking to that jerk? I thought he was in Italy filming a movie.

Desi: That's the thing. Lorenzo isn't your dad. Your dad is King Aung.

Floressa: Who?

Desi: The King of Tharma.

Floressa: Ha. That's funny. They didn't tell me you subs were comedians.

Desi: Floressa, I have never been more serious about anything in my life. They met when your mom was in *Once Upon an Island*, and she told him tonight.

Floressa: They don't even know each other.

Desi: It gets crazier. They were secretly married for a bit, but then the king's brother was assassinated and your mom ran away to America and had you.

Floressa: You're lying. You're joking. It's not funny anymore.

Desi: I'm sorry you had to hear it this way.

Floressa: Okay. Wait. How do you know?

Desi: Your mom told me . . . told you about it tonight.

Floressa: So now he wants to meet me?

Desi: Um . . . no.

Floressa: What do you mean no?

Desi: He already met you. At dinner tonight.

Floressa: And . . .

Desi: I think he was shocked. He didn't take it well.

Floressa: How could he not take it well? I'm Floressa
Chase.

Desi: Like I said, it was kind of dramatic.

Floressa: OMG, so this makes me a princess.

Desi: Technically, yes.

Floressa: That is so cool. Except the part where my dad
doesn't want me. And the part where you're with my
boyfriend.

Desi: I've never been alone with him. His brother, Karl, was
there the whole time.

Floressa: Oh, Karl. That kid is dullsville.

Desi: He's super nice, actually.

Floressa: Are we talking about KARL still? Who cares?
My dad is a king and he doesn't want me and . . . Oh, this
actually sucks. I have to go lie down.

Desi: Wait! You need to come to Tharma.

Floressa: No way. I'm not ready yet. I still need to think
about this.

Desi: What? Floressa, what am I supposed to do?

Floressa: Nothing. Do nothing. Don't tell anyone about this.

Sit tight and avoid everyone until I'm ready. Give me some

time and don't text me. I'll text you.

Desi: But what if something happens?

Floressa: Don't let it. Bye.

Gina woke me up at five the next morning. For once, she didn't look like an airbrushed image. Instead, her eyes were red, her face swollen. I rolled over, exhausted from a night spent tossing and turning. "Need to sleep," I said.

"The secret is out."

"I know it's out." I pulled my blanket under my chin. "You already told me."

"You weren't the only one spying in the garden." Gina picked up my clothes from the night before and folded them on a chair. "A paparazzo was there and he recorded the conversation. My publicist just called me— *Star Reporter Daily* is printing the story today."

Don't let anything happen, Floressa said. Yeah, well, *whoops*.

"Now what?" I asked.

"The best defense is a good offense. We're doing interviews at noon," she said.

"Interviews?" I buried my head under a pillow. "No. No, we aren't doing that."

"Flossie, I know this is hard, but if we spin it right, this could be positive press."

"Spin it? This isn't a story. This is my *life*."

"And part of your life is being in the public eye. I'm sorry, but you have to take the good and the bad." Gina frowned. "I'm flying in Brenda Waters to do it. I feel like I connected with her during our Oscar interview, and she's fabulous at making the interviewee look sympathetic."

"What does the king think about this?"

"I don't know. He's not talking to me. I've left messages, but he's already said he's going to deny everything. Brenda Waters reached out to him too, so maybe that will help."

I rubbed the sleep out of my eyes. "I thought you were going to give me time with this."

"Honey, either we tell our story or the media tells their version of it." She pushed a hair out of my face "I'm sorry. Get in the shower. I'll send for Ryder. Maybe even keep your skates on. It could add a little innocence to your image. We need you to be as likeable as possible, in case the king does counter press."

Once Gina left the room, I checked my manual. I'd written three texts so far to Meredith, but all of them had gone unanswered. I scrolled through the applications and paused when I thought about Genevieve's card. I could contact her. I would be out of here pronto, and Floressa would be back in time to lace up her own skates.

But what would that mean for Meredith? Would she get in trouble for not answering my texts? And there was that rumor about promotions; I didn't want her to look bad. And Floressa . . . would it be even worse for her to be catapulted into this situation without warning? No, I could at least tell her about the interview and give her the morning to mentally prepare. Meanwhile, I'd get Flossie dolled up for her return.

I typed the texts, musing that I had never used the letters ASAP so much in my life. After hiding my manual again, I showered and was brushing the tangles out of Floressa's hair when Ryder fluttered in, squeezing a notebook of some sort in his shaking hands.

"A fun mother-daughter getaway," he said. "That's what I was supposed to prepare for. Maybe, *maybe* a shot by the paparazzi here or there, but an interview with Brenda Waters? News that will make national—no INTERNATIONAL— headlines! That takes months, months to prepare for!"

I guided him into a chair. "It'll be all right."

"All right? *All right!*" Ryder flung the book across the room. It banged against the wall and flopped onto the bed. "This is a career-defining moment and I don't have an ounce of taffeta at my disposal."

I leafed through the book. Photos of Floressa in different outfits were pared with sketches and swatches of fabric. A bright, exotic, floral print caught my eye. I knew in a moment it was perfect. In this, with her hair long and flowing, there would be no denying Floressa was island royalty. She wouldn't have to say a thing. The dress would say it for her. "Do you have this fabric?"

"Sure. Bought that last season in Hong Kong."

"Do you think you could whip something together with it?"

Ryder narrowed his eyes. "You sure it's not too . . . too? You're going to fit right in with this, not stand out."

"Oh, I'll still stand out." I thumbed through some of the designs, an idea taking shape as I noted the items in Floressa's wardrobe. I'd come a long way from designing T-shirts. "Did you bring those earrings?" I pointed to a pair of delicate gold-and-coral hoops.

Ryder shrugged.

I nudged him with my elbow. "You know, I am a designer too."

"So?"

"So it's not like you're dressing a mannequin. We combine my fashion sense and your design skills and . . . Ryder, you're right. This *will* be career defining. We're going to make me look like an island princess. No one will be able to deny who I really am."

Ryder's eyes widened. "Can we use that gold belt I love?"

"Belt away."

"Come then, my princess." Ryder jumped up. "Your subjects await!"

It took three hours to get me properly polished. Ryder whipped up a dress using the fabric I'd found, and together we accessorized Floressa.

Gina sent in her PR team to brief me on what to say. I was supposed to play the clueless daughter who'd always wanted a father. And I had to cry—Brenda Waters made everyone cry. I wrote down everything. I wouldn't be answering these questions. Floressa would be back by then. She had to be.

I was alone in my bedroom organizing the notes when my manual zinged with news from both Meredith and Floressa. Ha! No Brenda Waters tears after all.

> Desi,
> My reception has been bad, so I barely saw this. I think you're going overboard with the ASAP. We already knew she was a royal—that's why she qualified for a sub. I've personally contacted Floressa concerning the matter, and she's asked us not to intervene. As a Level Two, her desires take precedence over Façade's usual protocol. Besides, you've been trained—take care of it and let me finish up this vacation. And DON'T contact Genevieve. That would make us both look bad.
> Hang in there. AND NO KISSING.
> Ta-ta,
> Meredith

Kissing? There was much heavier stuff going down here than *kissing*. Instead of monitoring this job or trusting a valued employee, Meredith was listening to Floressa, WHO WASN'T EVEN HERE. Floressa had no idea how big this was. Brenda Waters was on her way to make me bawl on international television!

I didn't bother to write her back. A cyborg had obviously taken over my agent's body. How I missed workaholic

Meredith. What was she doing that was *so* important anyway? If I messed this interview up, it wouldn't just impact royal circles. Everyone in America—heck, everyone who owned a TV—would know about it.

But it got worse. Much, much worse. Enter: Floressa's text.

Floressa: I'm not coming back.

I squeezed my eyes shut. Did Floressa and Meredith have a Let's Make Desi Go Crazy party? Were they sitting together laughing right now? Because *this* was bananas.

Desi: What?

Floressa: I'm sick. I have a stomachache. Can't leave.

Desi: You have to come back.

Floressa: No, I'm sick. My stomach feels weird.

Desi: Did you throw up?

Floressa: Eww, no. Okay, so I'm probably fine. But I'm not coming back.

Desi: It's nerves. I can relate, but you should get back for this interview. The questions are going to be personal. It would help if the person answering was YOU.

Floressa: I don't care about the interview anymore. I don't care about anything.

Desi: I know this is hard.

Floressa: I'm not coming back ever. There is no way I can see my dad after what he did. And my mom! My mom lied to me my whole life. This resort is super posh. I'm going to stay.

Desi: I don't know if that's an option.

Floressa: I'm rich. I can make anything an option. Barrett can even visit, since he's royal. Now go live my life for me and leave me alone.

Desi: Floressa, seriously, I think if you come back, you can make it through this. You have your mom and Barrett and your design stuff and . . . a life! A fabulous LIFE!

Three minutes later . . .

Desi: Floressa? R U there?

Five minutes later, Barrett knocked on the door. "Babe, I think they want to freshen up your makeup again before the interview."

"Yeah, coming."

Desi: Floressa, I'm going to this interview, and then we are going to work this out. You know you can't leave forever. Façade won't let you. I won't let you.

I added three frowny faces at the end. There I was, trying to help her, and she'd completely checked out on me. She couldn't stay at the resort. Every princess returns sometime.

Um. I think.

Chapter
20

Of course I knew Floressa Chase was famous. I'd seen her name and face plastered on countless magazines; I'd watched dozens of her interviews. If I wanted to, I could even buy my own Floressa Chase doll. But no amount of BEST could have prepared me for what it was like to *be* Floressa Chase.

Maybe that's where the obsession with celebrity stems from anyway. You think of this life, you build it up, and even the person living in it can't meet the ideal everyone has set. Floressa still had fears and sadness. Heck, she even had stomach problems.

Which I certainly could relate to, at least the stomach-ache part, as I watched the mass of paparazzi camped outside our yacht. The number of people on the small island had doubled overnight. If I'd thought the school play was going to be scary, this had to be a million times worse. There were cameras filming. And I had on roller skates. One flub and E! would be replaying it for weeks.

I closed the curtains in the sky lounge—the luxurious main-level space easily twice the size of my family's living room. It seemed like months ago that Gina and I had relaxed on the overstuffed leather couches, discussing her early movie career. Now we all waited for Gina to make her entrance so we could start our escape-to-interview plan. Ryder did one more makeup stroke and spritzed me with perfume.

"No one will smell me," I said.

"You will. And that essence will exude in your interview."

Barrett laughed at a video on his cell phone. He held it up. "This guy on a motorcycle crashed into a puppy. It's hilarious."

Prince Charming.

Karl sat at the wet bar, drinking grape juice and eating pretzels. This might be the last time I talked to him. Or worse, I could be Floressa for the rest of her (and my!) life, and Karl would always be my boyfriend's little brother.

I patted Barrett's knee. "I'm thirsty. You want a drink?"

"No thanks, babe, I'll stay here. The lighting works for me. Which one do you think is my good side, by the way?"

"Uh, hard to choose."

"You're right." He rubbed his chin. "They're both good."

I left Barrett to his lighting and wheeled over to Karl.

He had that same tormented look on his face from last night. The same look on his face from the night in Metzahg when we'd kissed. I grasped the edge of the bar to stop myself from grabbing his hand. Plus, it's always a smart idea to hold tight with roller skates, a rocking boat, and weak knees.

"Doing any better than yesterday?" I asked.

"Better is relative." He ran his finger over the lip of his cup. "How are *you* doing, that's the question. It's not every day you find out you're a princess."

That was the question, the question Barrett had neglected to ask Floressa all morning, even though the reason he and Karl had come by was to help us deal with the press. "It's a lot to have dropped on me at once."

"I would imagine. Actually, I can't imagine what it would be like. It's like . . . the world as you knew it has changed now."

Man, he was deep. "You're right," I said. "But I've been talking about it all morning. I'm going to talk about it all afternoon. I need a break."

"Understood."

"So let's talk about you instead."

"I'm not a very interesting topic at the moment."

"Are you kidding me? You've got that weird love triangle going for you." Or love rhombus if I added myself. Love . . . trapezoid? "Is that why you broke up with your girlfriend?"

Karl turned to appraise me. "Wow. You cut right to the chase."

"It's my last name."

"Well . . ." He rubbed at his eyebrow. "This makes me a terrible cad, but . . . the tabloids are actually true. I did break up with Olivia. For Elsa."

"That doesn't make you a cad." I stopped on the word. Who talks like that anyway? Karl was more formal than I remembered. "You went with the advice you gave me last night. Follow your heart."

"True." Karl ran his thumb along his jaw. "But now that Elsa knows how I feel, it's like this new piece of me is exposed. I'm not accustomed to it. It's exhilarating, but it's terrifying."

"Oh." So that basically summarized how I felt. About Karl. Liking someone you know you'll never have, or that you're not supposed to have, does cause this . . . this ache. I glanced out the one open window at the growing crowd and realized my time with Karl—if I could really call it *time with Karl*—was almost done. And I had to know if what I'd had with him before—when we'd spent the day together in Metzahg—was real. So I could hang on to it. So I could do what I needed to do.

Let go.

But I couldn't just come out and confess everything. I'd start with a hint. A reminder of our conversation as Karl and Elsa. We'd both professed a love for the 1940s movie *Casablanca*. It wasn't a film that teenagers often, if ever, quoted. An easy start.

"So . . . *Of all the gin joints in all the towns in all the world, she walks into yours*. Right?"

218

"I'm sorry . . . what?"

"It's a movie line. From *Casablanca*. You know, *Here's looking at you, kid?*"

"I've never seen it." Karl sipped his grape juice. "I'm not one for the cinema."

"Really? You sure?" I tried to keep my voice from going shrill. "Humphrey Bogart?"

"Is he an actor? Sports star of some sort?"

He'd just broken up with his girlfriend. He had to be distraught . . . forgetful. Because the last time I talked to him (as Elsa), he was quoting *Casablanca* lines with ease. It made no sense.

Unless he had been doing that to impress Elsa. Or was he lying now? He could be a liar. How well did I really know him, anyway? For the last two days he'd been stiff and forlorn. Which is understandable, sure, but where was the funny conversationalist I'd gotten to know in the garden? Did he only turn that on for Elsa?

Gina marched into the sky lounge, her beautiful features already set in her for-the-media smile. "Time to go, Flossie."

"Do you need help getting up the stairs?" Karl asked, all chivalry. "Don't want you to take a spill in front of the press."

I took his arm, resisting the urge to lean in too much. Karl was a good person. And he was honest. And I did feel something for him. Even though he was different on this job, our day together had been special, and nothing erased

219

that. As Humphrey Bogart said in his famous last line to Ingrid Bergman, *We'll always have Paris* (well, Metzahg, but whatever).

Barrett caught up with us at the top of the stairs. He nodded at Karl and wordlessly took my hand. "Good idea, brude," he said. "We'll be far more distracting on the dock. Let's fake fight and let the girls rush to the limo. If we get enough cameras pointed our way, Gina and Floressa might make it through that wave of people."

I couldn't imagine ever getting through the solid wall of onlookers. Our bodyguards circled around us as we walked/skated down the ramp. Once we were on the dock, Barrett pecked my cheek. "Good luck. You gonna miss me?"

I looked past him to Karl, who grimaced as flash after flash went off.

"Yeah. Yeah, I am."

"That's my girl. Now watch this." Barrett winked at me before shoving Karl. Although Karl knew they were faking a fight, the blow caught him off guard and he hit the ground. Sure enough, the cameras swiveled just long enough for Gina and me to slip into the waiting limo and swerve around the crowd. Some photographers scrambled to their cars, but we left the bulk of the crowd—and the dueling princes—behind.

The PR people inside the limo gave us the latest briefing. *Royal News Today* had broken the story that morning, and now news programs around the world were sharing and speculating. Our interview with Brenda Waters would be aired live—the sooner the better, as far as damage control went.

Gina had found us a hillside mansion for the interview. We would stay there until we could find a way off the island. The house was chosen partially for the scenery, but mostly because of the intense security—and dense jungle—surrounding it.

The place was already packed with crews: camera crew, makeup crew, lighting crew, the guys-in-suits-on-their-cellphones crew, and of course, Brenda Waters's crew. Add Gina's crew to the mix and that's a whole lot of crew going on.

The balcony overlooked the lush green mountains and ocean. Despite the insanity around me, I took a moment to lean against the railing and take in the view. In all my princessy traveling, I'd never seen anything like it.

"Hold it." Gina's personal photographer snapped my picture. "Perfect. Reflective and wistful. We'll use that for print interviews."

Why did every moment, especially this personal moment, have to be documented to prove that Floressa was human? Couldn't she just *be* human? All those people out there salivating over her story would expect—no, *demand*—alone time if their life fell apart like this. Instead, they were gleefully watching every second. It made me sick.

The balcony door slid open. "Flossie?" Gina wrapped her arms around me. "They're ready for us."

"I don't know if I'm ready for them."

She kissed me on the forehead. "I'll be right next to you.

You don't have to say anything. Actually, the less you talk, the more sad you'll seem, and it will appeal to the viewers—"

I brushed past Gina and into the interview room. I doubted Floressa would care about her image right now—the girl was so upset, she was willing to give up everything rather than face this. The makeup crew rushed over to brush, fluff, and spray. I waved them off and sat down on the couch, across from Brenda Waters.

She leaned over and patted my hand. "Thank you for granting me this interview."

"I didn't have much of a choice."

"I'll make sure you're depicted well."

"And I'll make sure I cry at some point, since it's apparently what the people want."

Brenda nodded, oblivious to my sarcasm. Gina joined me on the couch and gave my knee a squeeze. Someone adjusted a light so it was right in my face. A mike was attached to my dress, my makeup was fixed *again*, and then the camera guy counted down to zero and pointed at Brenda. A red light went on, and we were live. Live across the entire country. No, across the world.

"I'm Brenda Waters from *PulsePoint News*, talking to you live from Tharma. With me are Gina and Floressa Chase, whose recent family scandal was leaked to the world. Let's air the raw footage."

A TV by the teleprompter showed the paparazzo tape. The images of the king and Gina were grainy, but the sound was clear. Gina cringed when the king stormed away, then pasted on a weak smile before the camera went back on her.

"That was hard to watch, Brenda."

"I'm sure it was hard to *endure*."

I know when you're being interviewed, you're supposed to look at the person interviewing you, but the red light above the camera kept diverting my attention. Behind that lens, millions of viewers were watching this very private moment. They shouldn't be a part of it. *I* shouldn't be a part of it. Floressa would see this and regret that her reactions, her authentic emotions, were not the ones being played out on the screen.

Brenda went on with her condolences. "It must be so difficult to have your private tragedy broadcast to the world."

"It's been an extreme trial," Gina said.

I wanted to point out that *Brenda* had broadcast the footage too, but I knew the point would be lost.

"This too shall pass." Brenda leaned over to pat Gina's hand. Gina dabbed at her eyes. I scrunched lower on the couch.

I'd seen this all before. This story—a royal scandal—was told in tabloids over and over again. This story was a prime example of why tabloids even existed. And I'd always read the gossip before, with a sick kind of curiosity. I'd even found old interviews and newspaper articles about my favorite screen sirens, exposing their secrets long after they'd died. And now, looking into the hollow camera lens, I started to shake because I finally understood how it felt to live life on a stage.

"How have these recent events brought you two closer together?" Brenda asked.

I couldn't help it. I snorted.

Gina slipped her arm around me. "I don't think it has brought us closer, but I hope eventually it will. I didn't handle things right. This is all news to Floressa, just like it's news to the king. I was trying to protect her, and in the process, I hurt her. I hope this country and the viewers will forgive me for my shortcomings, and support Floressa during this difficult time."

"What a sacrifice that must have been, to expose your heart like that," Brenda said.

A tear slipped down Gina's cheek. I couldn't tell if it was genuine or not, but the cameraman was sure eating it up.

"Floressa!" Brenda said brightly, making it evident that this was now the sunny portion of her interview. "What is it like finding out that you're living every girl's dream come true?"

"What dream would that be, Brenda? Because this feels more like a nightmare."

"Right." Brenda flinched. "What I mean is, you're not only the daughter of a beloved Academy Award–winning actress, but . . . a princess!"

She said the word "princess" like it was *exciting*. Like this revelation was Floressa's fairy-tale ending.

I tore my eyes away from the camera, looking at Brenda first, then Gina, then at the people behind the camera. The publicist pointed to her mouth, indicating that I should smile big. The cameraman zoomed in with the hope that I would show some "authentic" emotion so the viewers would feel empathy.

Empathy.

Empathy.

Yes! That's it. With all the world staring at me, I finally figured out that my emotion, my magical emotion, was empathy. And although nothing outwardly magical happened (wouldn't it be cool if I could cry magical tears and wash Brenda Waters away?), the buzzing feeling hit me like a wave.

When my nerves and emotions and thoughts were close to exploding, I *was* feeling magic.

Boom.

Those moments of tingling—home life or subbing life—were all connected.

Boom.

I understood where the buzzing came from.

Boom.

My magic tuned in when I truly put myself in someone else's shoes, to the point that I could almost read their mind—no, read their *heart.* When I did that I became aware of exactly what they needed. My empathy served as an emotional, magical compass. And I clearly knew—KNEW—that Floressa wanted to move forward with her mom and build a relationship with her father *away* from the spotlight.

This interview could not go on.

Once again, I faced a decision that could very well cost me my job. I could see Meredith's finger wagging at me already, but the consequences didn't matter as much as this feeling. I had to do what was best for Floressa.

If Floressa ever wanted to get past her pain, she had to experience this drama for herself. And I had to go to the resort and bring her back so she could do that.

I stood up. "I can't do this right now."

Brenda, Gina, and the whole TV crew watched me in shock. I used their delayed reaction to my advantage and skated out of the living room, out the front door, and down the big winding driveway to the dense woods behind the house.

Once I hit dirt, I chucked off my skates and ran until I was far enough into the jungle that I wouldn't be instantly spotted. I crouched down next to a gnarly tree and yanked out my manual, stopping for a second when I thought of Meredith. She wasn't going to be happy when she found out I'd contacted Genevieve. I'd have to figure out a cover story for her later. Right now, I was dizzy with the need to help Floressa.

"Genevieve! Genevieve! I would like to summon Genevieve!"

Her assistant, Dominick, appeared on my screen. "Dominick, I need help."

Dominick spoke. "Genevieve is unavailable at the moment. She is preparing for her birthday celebration. If you would like to leave a message—"

"No message! I've got a major royal scandal going on, I can't get ahold of my agent, there is a TV crew looking for me, and . . . magic! I know all about my magic!"

"—then please do so at the beep." Dominick smiled and I realized it was a recorded message, that he hadn't heard a word I said. "Beep," he added.

I hung up. There had to be some application on this manual that could help me. I scrolled through until I found a picture of a bubble. Emergency bubble.

EMERGENCY BUBBLE APPLICATION

Agents typically send emergency bubbles when subs must retreat quickly. There are rare occasions, however, when a sub must remove herself from a situation. At such times, the sub can summon an emergency bubble to take her to the agency or next destination for help. This is not a feature to be used lightly, as emergency bubbles are difficult to navigate, and although the Law of Duplicity can be employed, some timing issues involving the princess's absence may arise. If the sub still finds her circumstance to be dire, an emergency bubble can be summoned by clicking HERE.

I clicked on the HERE and a form came up, asking me why I needed the bubble, how long I would need it, what my insurance information was, what bubble navigational system I preferred—

Someone, someone close, called Floressa's name. I rushed through the information, and within seconds of hitting SUBMIT, I heard a sputtering in the tree bark. It oozed sap, and from that sap, a bubble gargled out, which grew into a clunky orb.

There wasn't a permeable wall like in Meredith's bubble. I had to twist open the creaky hatch and let myself in. And just in time. The voices were near when I shut the door, safe with the invisibility provided by MP.

The bubble was all knobs and dials, like a single-engine plane. Well, maybe it was like a single-engine plane—not that I'd ever been in one. What I did know was that I had no clue how to steer the thing. I jiggled a few of the knobs, but nothing happened.

I opened drawers, looking for some manual. Manual. Duh. I clicked around FAQ until I found the HOW TO FLY AN EMERGENCY BUBBLE section.

Which was about a hundred pages long. The thing was a *textbook* that would require weeks to get through. I had, like, minutes.

I hit my head on the dash. I was stuck. Stuck living someone else's life for them. I would NEVER get to be in that play now. I'd never even turn fourteen. Or see my family or friends or sit around in pajamas without worrying about my picture being taken.

I forced away my own problems and focused on the mess Floressa was in. I brushed angrily at my tears. Becoming a princess always *solved* the problems in fairy tales, it didn't create them! What was going to happen to Floressa now?

"This isn't fair to Floressa!" Through my tears, I hit the

dash and started to scream, "Fly, you stupid thing! WHY DON'T YOU FLY?"

The bubble rose in the air, dipping up and down. "It's flying," I whispered to myself. "IT'S FLYING!" I jumped up and did a happy dance dorky enough that I prayed there wasn't some sort of surveillance video watching me. I completed my gleeful shuffling and positioned myself in the pilot seat. The bubble's steering wheel looked like one from an airplane, and I tipped it down. The bubble rose. Flight! I had made this happen.

Now I just needed to . . . go. "Uh, Bermuda Triangle? Façade Resort."

The bubble shook, as if nodding in agreement, and flew up and forward. My sadness seeped away, though I was still jittery from my crying episode. Once the bubble steadied, I skimmed to the end of the instructions, checking that my transportation wasn't actually possessed and steering me to the bowels of the earth. I read the very last line.

Of course, for experienced subs, there is always that Magical Option. Channel your MP and autopilot will take over, steering you where you want to go. Few have the skills to employ this, but if you do, sit back and enjoy the ride.

That Magical Option. I'd used it—used magic to do something besides look like a royal. The bubble worked as soon as I turned my thoughts to Floressa, felt empathy for her. My magic worked if I was using it on someone's behalf.

I leaned back in my chair. This was the first manual mention, albeit vague, of a sub's ability to employ magic beyond Royal Rouge. Did I need Rouge *and* my magical emotions to employ the magic? Or was the Rouge not necessary? I'd experienced the same feeling when I'd helped Celeste, after all. If this was the case, Genevieve really had lied. Good thing she didn't answer my call.

I still didn't understand *why* Façade kept magical information from subs, why they were hiding the magic under their top hat. I mulled this over for most of the long bubble ride—no warp speed with this clunker. The bubble hit turbulence thirty minutes or so in, the radar indicating entrance into the Bermuda Triangle. I held on to the bottom of my seat when the bubble began its descent. My ride may have been on autopilot, but did it have auto-land?

It did. Really junky auto-land. The bubble bumped and skidded a few times, nearly crashing before it stopped. I cracked my licorice-twisted neck. Another thing to check in the manual—disability insurance. The hatch resisted my first few pushes, but finally groaned open.

We'd landed, all right. Right on the most beautiful beach I had ever seen in my life. And I had seen it before— as a much more scaled-down version. Scaled down, like, to model size.

Chapter
21

Sometime during the landing, the Rouge wore off, switching me back to my Titania costume. Part of me wanted to lie down and enjoy the tropical setting, especially after my panic attack, but I knew being around my client *while* I was subbing for her had to be messing up some sort of time rules. I picked my way up a dirt path that twisted into dense palm trees. Hidden behind those was the resort.

The model didn't do it justice. It's not like it was a monstrous resort—the size was much closer to the Holiday Inn Express we had in Sproutville. But this was a royal hideaway, and so the luxury meter was at full throttle.

Elegant and comfortable, the island-themed lobby incorporated all the natural beauty of the outside landscaping into the sleek design. It looked like the hotel could serve hundreds, but no one was there. Even the front desk was empty. I rang the crystal-encrusted bell, and a man poked his head out. He smiled, and wow—he looked like a young Will Smith.

"Can I help you?" He emerged from the back room and stood behind the desk. I couldn't answer at first because his resemblance was more than a similarity. He *was* Will Smith, Will Smith early in his career. Maybe . . . maybe it was his son? But why would his son work at Façade Resort? The guy probably heard about the uncanny resemblance all the time and got sick of it. I decided to play it cool and not bring it up.

"Um, yeah. I'm looking for a guest."

"We don't release the whereabouts of our guests. Company privacy policy."

I rested on the counter and lowered my voice. "Look . . . what's your name?"

"Will."

"Of course it is. Will, I'm on a top secret Level Two mission. I would tell you more, but you don't have clearance to hear it. I flew in via emergency bubble and I'm in a time crunch. Can you please tell me where Floressa Chase is so I can finish saving her life?"

Will glanced around the empty lobby. "Are you her sub?"

"Yes."

"I'm going to have to check that out. Let me pull up the file and I'll ask you some questions."

Will tapped for a minute on his keyboard and glanced up at me. "Name?"

"Desi Bascomb."

"Age? Birth date?"

"Thirteen. Well, fourteen on December tenth."

"What is your greatest fear, Desi?"

I blinked. "They don't have that in the computer."

"I would think any employee, especially a Level Two, would realize that Façade knows *everything*."

"Fine. Um . . . being invisible. And big dogs."

Will asked me a few more personal questions, and I tried not to squirm. Floressa owed me huge for my efforts. Like throw-in-your-yacht *huge*.

Finally, Will punched one more key and offered the charming smile that had made him famous. I mean, the *celebrity* famous.

"I can't tell you the room, but I can tell you she's by the pool bar."

"Great." I grabbed a mint from the bowl on the counter. "I'll go find her."

"Desi?"

I turned back around. "Huh?"

He pointed at a door to the left of the front desk. "Don't forget your makeup before you go out there. You shouldn't even be walking around without it."

I looked down at my fairy costume. New clothes I could use, but makeup? I already had on the thick stage stuff, and besides, who cared about *makeup* when both Floressa Chases were here, meaning NO ONE was next to that old tree on the island.

I pushed open the door and nearly choked on my mint. The room was a mini-version of the Glamourification Studio's makeup display, divided into two sections: the regular makeup, and a much larger selection of the Old Hollywood line. I saw newer names—like Meryl Streep Base Powder and Sandra Bullock Blush, but also a whole area filled with old starlets. Some of the slots were empty, like Marilyn Monroe, Doris Day, Grace Kelly . . . Maybe those were popular. I uncorked a Julie Andrews Poppy Red and rubbed it on my lips. The lipstick tingled like this expensive collagen plumping stuff my mom uses. There were no mirrors anywhere on display. Weird, but really, what *wasn't* weird here?

I fumbled through my purse for my Rouge compact. The mirror inside was dirty, so I wiped it on my costume. I held it up to see my lips and almost screamed.

Looking back at me was not Desi Bascomb, or even Floressa Chase. I had transformed into Julie Andrews. Julie Andrews as she looked in the movie *Mary Poppins*, complete with bun, hat, and gray suit.

Will poked his head in. "Oh, good. You've transformed. Nice umbrella, by the way."

By my side, sure enough, was my umbrella. Maybe if I opened it up, I could fly away to Normalville. I looked up at Will, and that's when things clicked. "This makeup makes everyone . . ." I paused. I was now speaking in an eloquent

British accent. "Makes everyone at the resort look and *sound* like the name on the bottle."

"Well, usually. One time there was a mix-up when I put on some Lon Chaney for Halloween—you know, he was the original Phantom of the Opera in a silent movie—and I ended up looking like Jim Carrey from *The Mask*. But still. Cool costume."

For an agency that prided itself on privacy, it made perfect sense. Multiple royals would be here at the same time. To avoid revealing which royals had subs, the agency made all the royals look like someone else. The fact that they looked like celebrities was probably loads of fun for them—escaping and playing pretend. Don't a lot of celebrities use fake names when they check into hotels anyway? Façade took it further. Much, much further.

Of all the ways to use magic, this was where Façade focused its energy. Some poor girls got their magic ripped away if they didn't "measure up," while royals got to play dress-up. It wasn't right. As soon as I cleaned up Floressa's mess, Meredith and I were going to have a serious talk.

I spread my hand along the rows of empty slots. "So all the empty ones are being used."

"We restock them once the guest checks out. The ladies get catty if someone steals their look."

My eyes were drawn to the Marilyn Monroe slot. So Floressa. "Thanks. I think I know who I'm looking for now."

Will stepped out of the doorway so I could pass. "Hey, Mary?"

I kept walking.

"Mary Poppins . . . er, Julie Andrews."

"What?"

"You forgot your umbrella." He held it out for me, a goofy smile on his face. I grabbed it and beelined to the pool, the wool suit already making me sweat. Dang, why hadn't I picked someone else? Annette Funicello, star of sixties beach movies, would at least have a bathing suit on.

Floressa, a.k.a. Marilyn, was sunning by the pool in her signature fifties-style white bathing suit. I dragged a chair over and plopped down next to her. She lowered her sunglasses and smiled.

"Have I been a bad girl?" she asked in Marilyn's sweet, high voice. "Do I need a nanny?"

I shoved the umbrella onto the seat next to me and leaned forward on my knees. "I feel like I *am* your nanny, actually, Floressa."

"Hey, I'm in disguise. You're not supposed to know that."

"I'm your sub. And I'm here to take you home."

Floressa sat up on her elbows. "If you're my sub, then who is being me?"

"Exactly."

"Well, you're not doing a very good job."

"I didn't sign up to do it for *life*."

"You shouldn't be complaining." Floressa stretched. "Most girls would love to be me."

The sun was beating down hard. I took off my coat and loosened my bun. "That's true. Because you have a great life,

Floressa. One you should go back to and live for yourself."

Floressa tore off her sunglasses and stared me down. "Just what do I have to get back to, exactly? The humiliation of knowing there's a father who doesn't want me?"

"I know it's tough. But what about the mother who loves you?"

She shrugged. "If she loved me, she would have told me about my dad."

"She did. She just did it late. Look, she planned this whole trip for you. And she is going to get all sorts of bad publicity for letting this info leak. She risked a lot for you. You're not the only one hurting, here. Besides, your dad has only had one day to digest this information. Maybe he'll come around."

"So . . ." Floressa tapped her finger to her plump lips. "You're saying if I go back, I'll still have a chance to be his daughter. To be royal?"

"You *are* royal. It's in your blood. That's why you were able to use this agency."

"Hmmmm . . . I always wanted to be a princess. I thought I would have to marry Barrett to get that."

"And there's Barrett! He's waiting for you with his brother, Karl."

"Who cares about Karl? That boy is such a bore."

"Is not!"

"Oh, so you like him?" Floressa readjusted her shades. "I know he was having issues with Olivia. I can set you two up. Um . . . are you pretty underneath that disguise?"

Set me up. This girl was classic. "I'm good, thanks."

"I'm still not convinced. They have yummy cheesecake here, you know."

"Fine. Stay, then," I said. "Eat your cheesecake and I'll go back to Barrett."

"What?"

"Well, if you never go back, I'm not going to be able to hold him off forever. He'll think you don't like him anymore. So I guess I'm going to have to kiss him. To maintain appearances, of course."

Floressa gave me an appraising look. "You're good."

"Thanks."

"Okay, fine. I'll go back. Let me go find the lady who signed in with me. Miranda."

"Meredith?" I asked, searching the pool deck. Meredith had been *here* all along? Was that why she wasn't answering my pleas for help? Someone needed a scolding from Miss Poppins, that's for sure.

"Yeah, although she's someone else now. There's not too many people checked in. You could try the spa . . . Maybe the pool bar."

The bar was far enough away that I couldn't make out the two people sitting there. I stood. "Why don't you relax while I arrange your ride home?"

"Uh-huh. Hey, you're blocking my sun."

I opened up my umbrella for shade. Too bad I couldn't make it fly. That would be some entrance.

When I was close enough to see who it was, I smiled.

Grace Kelly was laughing loudly at something Frank Sinatra, her costar in Meredith's favorite old movie, *High Society,* was whispering in her ear.

Frank Sinatra was a dreamboat, huh? Oh, she was so easy to figure out. I closed my umbrella and took a seat next to them.

"I'll have a strawberry lemonade, please," I said to the bartender. "And can you add a spoonful of sugar?"

Grace and Frank ignored me, absorbed in their own intimate world. I leaned over and said, "Top of the morning to you, Meredith."

Meredith swiveled in her chair, Grace Kelly's ice blue eyes wide. "Who are you?"

"Mary Poppins. Lovely to meet you." Ha! Disguises were fun.

Meredith pursed her lips. "Lilith?"

"Do you really think Lilith would go for Mary Poppins?"

"Desi." Meredith exhaled. "What are you doing here?"

The bartender brought me my drink and I took a sip. "That's a great question. Why don't you answer it?"

"I told you I had things to do."

"Right. And to only contact you in case of emergency. Which I did three times."

"What emergency?"

"Oh, just your classic case of Royal Deciding She's Never Coming Back. Ever."

"And you're here . . ."

"Via emergency bubble. To bring her back."

"What? DESI." Meredith glanced anxiously around the pool deck. "You're not supposed to do that."

"And you're not supposed to leave your subs stranded. I'm guessing the agency looks down on that too."

Meredith flopped her head down on the bar. "I forgot the charger for my manual."

"Uh-huh."

"And the reception is awful."

"Sure."

"This is why I never take vacations."

Frank rubbed Meredith's back. "Is everything going to be all right, darling?"

So, I knew Meredith had been talking to her prince, but I had no idea they were having secret vacations. It explained her recent behavior. It also made her incredibly human at this moment, even if she wasn't in her own human image. I would never reveal her secret—Meredith was a friend, in a tells-me-what-to-do-and-can-be-rude-and-sometimes-I-think-she-might-hate-me kind of way. But this was a situation I could fully use to my advantage, and I was not about to miss the opportunity.

I stretched my hand across the bar and offered it to Frank. "Hi! You must be Meredith's prince. I'm Desi, her favorite substitute."

Meredith shot up. "How do you know who he is?"

"You just told me."

Meredith grabbed my ruffled blouse. "If you ever tell ANYONE this, your career at Façade is over. My career at

240

Façade would be over. Please, Desi. This is the only way we can meet."

"I'm not going to tell anyone."

She loosened her grip.

"I'm not going to tell anyone, but you *are* going to tell me everything you know about magic."

Meredith fumed. "You know I can't do that."

"Oh, I think you can. And you will, in exchange for my silence."

"There's a reason you don't know things yet, Desi. You're safer that way."

"Safe from what? Doing some good? Just like what Façade should be doing instead of wasting it on Marilyn Monroe costumes."

"That's a big issue you're poking at," Meredith said.

"Well, I already poked enough to figure out my own magic."

"No, you didn't."

"Yes, I did."

"Did not."

"Did too."

"Did not." Meredith rubbed the bridge of her nose. "Stop. We're not going to argue about that now. This is what we're going to do. We'll take Floressa back. Genevieve's party is tonight, so everyone will be busy and I'll have an opportunity to show you some things. That's the best I can do."

"I'll take it." I hopped up from my seat. "Come find us when . . . when you're ready to go."

Meredith nodded miserably. I waved to Frank Sinatra, who gave me a quick bow. I'd covered half the pool deck when I turned back around. They were in the middle of a sweet farewell kiss, one that was movie worthy. I felt a pang of sympathy for Meredith, loving someone she couldn't be with. I would say it was the same with Karl, but it wasn't. My stint as Floressa showed me how little I really knew him. Karl was a great guy, sure, but he was Elsa's. I was okay with that. The next boy I liked would live in my country and actually know I *existed*.

The lovebirds pulled apart, and Meredith wiped at her eyes. I left them to their moment while I searched for Marilyn. Now I could ditch the emergency bubble for the luxury of Meredith's office. And rest my feet for a bit. Because, seriously, Mary's button-up shoes were *killing* me.

Chapter
22

We dropped Floressa off in Tharma, and Meredith flipped on her reception room TV. In the three hours since I'd jumped into the emergency bubble to find Floressa, the story had blown up. The king had sent out a search party, and every channel was filled with shots of the rescuers slashing through the jungle. Another station featured a hysterical Gina— "There were dozens of people on the set. How could she disappear? This is all my fault!"

One camera zoomed in on a blur. Floressa picking her way down a hill. Someone from the rescue party caught her and wrapped her in a blanket. A cheer went out. Brenda Waters rushed over with a camera. "Floressa! Floressa! What terrors did you see in that jungle?"

243

Floressa pushed the camera aside and gave her mother a hug. They sobbed, holding each other, a shot that would be rerun on every news station for weeks to come.

Meredith clicked off the screen. "The king didn't completely disown her if he's sending out a search party. There's hope there. You're going to get a strong PPR on that one."

"I didn't rescue her for a strong PPR."

I followed Meredith into her office. The red message light on her phone was beeping angrily. Every inch of desk space was covered in notebooks and paper. Meredith sighed. "This is why I don't take vacations. This work will have to wait—Genevieve's party is going on, so I guess it was best to leave . . . the resort when I did. It's a costume ball, so that fairy thing you have on should be fine. As for me . . ." Meredith pulled out a small black masquerade mask.

"Awesome! This will be my first agency event."

"No, it won't. We aren't going." Meredith snapped her mask over her face. "It's a cover. You wanted me to tell you more? Well, I'm going to show you. Step out of the bubble."

The lobby was vacant. "They're in the ballroom," Meredith whispered. "Follow me."

We twisted through hallways, away from the ones I recognized and into darker corridors. The royal decor thinned out until only an occasional tapestry hung along the stone walls. Finally we came to a white door. Meredith lifted a chain tucked around her neck, revealing an antique brass key. She slipped it into the lock and turned. She cut me a severe look. "Showing you this could get both of us fired. Got it?"

I made a sealed motion across my lips.

The cafeteria-size room was white. Like, come-into-the-light white. A few lab tables were spread out across the shiny floor. Nothing was on top of them. No one else was in the room.

"Is this . . . is this where the subs get sanitized?" I asked.

"No. This is." Meredith tapped the wall twice, and it rolled away, revealing rows and rows of built-in shelves crowded with hundreds of multicolored jars pulsing like lava lamps. In the middle of the rainbow was a vanity, similar to the one in my grandma's house. And like Grandma's, the counter was cluttered with crystal perfume bottles, a bronzed hairbrush and . . . Rouge. Meredith picked up the silver compact and rubbed the jade beetle on the lid. The same beetle I'd seen on Genevieve's card. "It's a scarab beetle. The Egyptian symbol of renewal."

"So is that, uh, age-defying makeup?" I asked. I knew that wasn't the answer. I wanted it to be, though.

"No. If you put this makeup on, your magic is . . ."

"Poof."

Meredith and I whirled around. Lilith lounged against a table, all smiles. She wore a purple dress with bell sleeves, a smocked bodice, and one of those heavy medieval head-dresses. "I assume you have your reasons for showing Desi this room."

"Obviously, Lilith."

"And those would be . . ."

245

"Like I'm going to tell you."

"Level Twos don't come in here anymore." Lilith pushed back a lavender curl. "Unless they're being sanitized."

I widened my eyes. "Mer, you aren't going to—"

"Of course not. And I told you not to call me Mer." She shot a look at Lilith. "We both know Desi isn't your average Level Two. She was given Genevieve's card."

"Seriously?" Lilith let her mouth drop before covering it with a sneer. "Well, you can explain it all to Genevieve. I'm going to report this right away."

Meredith rolled her eyes. "You are such a snitch."

"Are you trying to get on my good side? Because I must say you're failing."

"I'm tired of playing sides. And I'm tired of you. We'll come back when we can be alone. Come on, Desi."

Lilith blocked the door. "Of course you'll understand if I don't let you go. This information should guarantee me a promotion."

"Promote this." Meredith grabbed Lilith's sleeve and yanked down. The fabric ripped, and we all gasped. Lilith lunged for Meredith's mask, and within seconds they were clawing at each other on the floor. I wanted to help, but I couldn't risk my costume tearing. I grabbed the compact from the shelf and held it in the air.

"If you both don't stop right now, I'll . . . I'll throw this makeup."

Meredith and Lilith froze. Meredith inched toward me. "You have no idea what that can do—"

"Put it down," Lilith said. "Please, I won't tell."

They untangled themselves. I couldn't believe they were acting so, as Reed would say, *junior high*. Ripped clothes, messed-up hair . . . Lilith even had a scratch on her arm. My superiors. The scene would have been funny if it hadn't been so serious.

Of course, I wasn't going to do anything with the makeup, but I felt powerful holding it. So this was where they'd brought Fake McKenzie. This makeup took away her magic, took away a promising future. What did the other containers do, then? And what was with the rainbow jars? Was that the real secret Meredith was going to disclose? "I'll put down the makeup if you two . . . *make up*."

"Sorry." Meredith patted her hair. "That was uncalled for. I'm very passionate about my clients and work, and I lost it."

Lilith ripped off her other sleeve to match, and straightened her headdress. "I'm sorry, too." A wicked smile spread across her face. "Sorry you are both two seconds away from being fired."

She cracked open the door. Genevieve, dressed as Cleopatra, in a white robe with gold jewelry and a heavy headdress, was seething in the doorway. Her usually warm brown eyes blazed. "I sensed activity in here."

"So did I." Lilith pointed at us. "I found Meredith showing a Level Two the sub-sanitation room."

"I'm sure she had good cause." Genevieve shifted her piercing gaze from Lilith to Meredith.

"I did. But I would rather discuss that in private," Meredith said.

"Oh, please," Lilith said. "It's all out there now."

"Lilith, why don't you join the festivities downstairs? Tell them I'll return shortly. Specter arrived and they're already mucking up the place."

"But they were—"

"Thank you, Lilith."

Lilith stomped out of the room. Genevieve crossed the white space and motioned for me to hand her the compact. I did so, wordlessly, and she set it back on the shelf, which disappeared into the wall. "You don't want to touch that."

"I know. It takes away magic."

Meredith stepped forward. "She figured it out herself. I just filled in the cracks."

"That was a risky move, Meredith, especially if you believe the rumors of my retirement. Your promotion could be on the line."

"You gave her your card." Meredith shrugged. "You're obviously aware of her capabilities. She's the most accelerated sub I've ever had. It wasn't that much of a risk."

"Hi! Me! Here!" I pushed past them and sat on the white tabletop. "Would someone tell me what is going on?"

Genevieve touched a wall, and a doorknob appeared. Meredith looked as surprised as I was. Genevieve led us into a grandiose office, with thousands of crystals hanging from the ceiling. The windows looked out on the Paris night, the moonlight dancing through the crystals. Genevieve motioned to two chairs—make that *thrones*—facing a desk the size of Michigan. "I've allowed very few people into my office. I trust you'll keep its whereabouts to yourselves."

Meredith's eyes were the size of a Rouge compact. "I thought this place was a fable."

"We'll have to save the tour for another time." Genevieve waved her hand. "Now, Desi, I can make you a deal. You may inquire about that room if I may ask you about your magic. No lies."

"No lies?" I repeated. Genevieve tipped her head to the side. She could find out anything she wanted on her own. We both knew that. I wanted answers. "Deal. What was in those jars?"

"You don't mince words, do you?"

Meredith reached across her throne and patted my hand. I looked at her, but she was intent on Genevieve.

"Those jars are magical storage vessels," Genevieve said. "Once we sanitize sub hopefuls, we liquefy their magic until it can be synthesized into another material. That magic powers our bubbles, hides Façade within this building, runs central command . . . You get the idea."

"So, Façade is run on stolen magic."

"*Stolen* is a harsh word." Genevieve spread her hands across her desk. "Some of the magic is borrowed. Donated. When you become an agent, you don't need as much, so we have magic drives. But, yes, some of it is stripped from sub hopefuls."

"And you don't think that's evil?"

"There are many things in this world that are evil. Dictators. Genocide. Hate. I've seen what happens when a magical person uses her abilities to hurt others. So channeling unused magic to a worthier outlet? No, I don't find that evil."

I sat back and chewed on a nail. Okay, so evil was extreme. But bad. This was at least *bad*, right?

"Again," Genevieve said, "I trust this information will be kept quiet."

"You don't usually learn all of this until you're an agent," Meredith said softly.

Right. Who am I going to tell?

Genevieve leaned forward. "And now I have some questions. Have you had any tingling or buzzing since we last spoke."

"Yes."

"And why didn't you use my card?"

Meredith coughed.

I ran my hands along the arms of the throne. "I did try— at the end. Before that, I wasn't sure what was happening. You told me that subs cannot use magic without Rouge. That my experiences at home had nothing to do with magic. Remember?"

"I wasn't being deceitful. You're still very new with the agency, and this wasn't intelligence you were classified to know yet. But, as Meredith said, you have very strong MP, and so you've obviously learned a bit of magic's possibility on your own."

"We don't have magic *potential*, do we? It's magic. Straight magic."

"No, for most it remains simply potential. Some subs can't ever use magic without a boost provided by Rouge—alone, their MP isn't enough to transform. And until you master your emotional talent, it's not fully-fledged magic."

"I think I know mine." I told her about the play tryouts, about the realization at Floressa's interview. "That's when it clicked for me. My connecting emotion is—" I paused before saying the word, not sure if I should share everything. I looked to Meredith, and she gave me a slight nod. "My emotion is empathy."

"Yes, I suspected as much." Genevieve rubbed her chin. "It practically drips off of you. I haven't seen anything like it in a long time. I've been watching you ever since Dorshire and . . . you're a very exciting substitute."

"Why?" I asked. "You guys keep talking like I'm the promised child. What makes empathy so special?"

Meredith shook her head. "It took me years, *years*, before I figured out my emotion."

"What's yours?" I asked.

"Kindness," Meredith said.

"Kindness?"

"Are you questioning me?"

Maybe it's a special talent she only reveals during a full moon. A full moon in a leap year. "No, um, it's just . . . Okay. Kindness."

"I'm totally kidding." Meredith broke into a fit of giggles. "Seriously, like I'm telling you another one of my secrets."

Genevieve cleared her throat. "Empathy gives you a natural edge. You can understand your client's needs more than anyone else. You don't need profiles or instructions or background checks. You're intuition is enough of a guide— we saw this happen during your Level One performances, and now again with Floressa. Empathy is a skill perfectly tailored to your position. And this talent makes you the ideal candidate to Match with an elite princess—to become her long-term substitute, a sub's greatest honor." Genevieve walked around to the front of her desk, taking my hand in hers. "Desi, what do you think of advancing to Level Three?"

I swallowed. "I didn't even know there was a Level Three."

"Oh, there is. You'd be one of very few teens to achieve it. You can Match at that level, take on agent-assistant duties— Well, you could find out more if you accept the promotion. And naturally, with Meredith leading you so well, I'd also offer her a new spot on the council."

"Council?" Meredith whispered. Her eyes glazed over, visions of council perks dancing in her head.

I curled up in the velvet chair. Genevieve had her own Wall o' Awesome Things behind her desk, except hers had every royal in the world mapped out, connected with strings and sheets of paper explaining their titles and connections. I would Match for one of those princesses, experience the royal treatment as I woke up in her lavish bed. I could travel the world, befriend Elsa, start a charity. . . . The whole room was awash with possibility.

But what about the other room, the one we'd just left? The room Fake McKenzie visited to have her magic removed. That was wrong. No matter what reason Genevieve gave me, it still seemed wrong that Façade would strip magic from anyone who didn't use MP as Façade saw fit. And the lie that the subs *always* needed the Rouge, *always* needed Façade for anything magical to happen, when in actuality it was possible to use our own magic as long as we figured out how. We didn't need Façade; Façade needed us. Yes, power should be balanced, but whose job was it to keep Façade in check?

Saying no wasn't a safe move, though. I knew what Façade and Genevieve were capable of. What would stop Genevieve from whisking me into the next room and bottling up my magic into a new nail polish shade? With one makeup application, my opportunity to impact anyone— royals or not—would be washed away. This promotion could be legit, or it could be a bribe. The only way to learn more was to stick with the agency.

Genevieve's phone rang, and she reached across her desk to pick it up. "Yes? Really? Those brutes." She placed her hand over the receiver. "Specter."

Meredith rolled her eyes.

"No, I'm almost done," Genevieve said into the phone. "Do not start the pie-eating contest without me."

She hung up. "I'm a slave to healthy competition. I must return to the festivities. Both of you consider the offer, and let me know as soon as possible. We *are* restructuring, although the rumor isn't true. I'm *not* retiring. This girl still has some tricks left." She hurried us out the office door.

Back in the sanitation room, Meredith's bubble was already waiting. Genevieve said, "I summoned it for you. So nice to chat, Desi. I know it's a lot to digest, but we are a respected, venerable, worldwide institution. There is much good you can accomplish with us. I trust you'll make the right choice."

I wasn't sure how much of a choice I had, but I waved good-bye to her and slipped into the bubble.

Meredith jumped onto her couch. "Council! *Council!*"

"That's great, Mer."

"I'm not even going to scold you for the *Mer*." She bounced around the pillows. "Mer. Mer. I don't care! Lilith is going to scream. After all these years, and COUNCIL!!"

"I'm, uh . . . going to leave you alone to celebrate."

I shut the door of Meredith's office. Not only did I have a lot of soul-searching to do, but there was a play starting as soon as I got home. If I thought about this too much right now—about the room and a promotion and empathy—I wouldn't have any space in my brain for my lines. I sat crossed-legged on the floor and worked on some of Gina's character-meditation exercises. If Mrs. Olman only knew.

Ten minutes later, Meredith floated into her office and rummaged through her desk. "Wait until he hears about this. I never dreamed I could make council. I could amend *laws* there."

I opened one eye. "Do you mean your prince?"

She stood behind her desk, manual in hand, her eyebrows knit together as she read something on her screen. Within seconds, Meredith fell to the floor. My all-business, hard-nosed agent had fainted.

I picked up her manual. The message on the screen had two simple words. Probably the only words that could be bigger than the council promotion.

MARRY ME.

I had to decide if I would stay with an agency I didn't fully trust. But Meredith's choice, it seemed, was a lot more epic than mine.

Chapter 23

Once I got her conscious, Meredith flew me home in record time. We didn't talk—didn't discuss the promotion or the text. She was visibly shaken, so I eased her onto the couch and had her sip water. When we landed, Meredith simply said, "We'll talk about what this means. Soon. Ta-ta, and break a leg."

I made sure no legs were broken as I slipped backstage. I was getting a headache. You'd think with all the products they manufactured, Façade could venture into magical sub medicine.

I elbowed my way into the busy dressing room to check that my face didn't look as shocked as I felt.

"Des! There you are." Kylee grabbed my arm. "I snuck

back to see you before the play starts. You look so beautiful."

I ran my fingers across the beads of my dress. I much preferred it to the Mary Poppins look. "You think so?"

"Absolutely. Although, wait . . ." Kylee rummaged through her purse until she found a purple plastic compact. Ah, how simple my life was when makeup was only makeup. "This will cover up the shine. And you might want to find some blush. You're looking pale."

Mrs. Olman yelled backstage. "Actors! Fifteen minutes!"

"You're mom is saving me a seat. Did you make her the shirt she's wearing?"

"No, is it mine?" I asked

"It says *Team Desi*. Your dad and Gracie have them too."

The news poured over me like warm maple syrup. My family was solid. Real. Here, in Idaho. Never before had I been so happy for the *normalc*y of my life.

"And, hey," Kylee said, "I wanted to give you a good-luck hug."

A true friend gives you exactly what you need, even if she has no idea why you need it. I hugged Kylee back, squeezing my eyes shut while tears slipped onto her shoulder. Kylee finally drew back and gave me a puzzled look.

"You okay?"

I brushed away a tear. "Yeah. Just . . . it's been a long day. It's a big day."

"Here. You have a little mascara—" Kylee wiped my cheeks. "I know this is tough, but this is your moment. Drink it up, 'kay?"

I nodded. "Too bad I don't have Reed's donkey head. Then I could cry all I wanted."

"Speaking of, I saw him a second ago."

"Yeah? Did you talk?"

"No. You know what?" Kylee blew at a bang. "I don't know if it's worth feeling like this. I get so nauseous every time he's around. I'd have to buy stock in Pepto-Bismol if we ever went out."

"But you two would be so cute together."

"Maybe. I don't know." The houselights flickered. "Why are we even talking about this? Go do jumping jacks, or whatever you theater geeks do to get ready."

"Kylee . . . thanks."

She gave me one more quick hug. "Go Team Desi."

Titania wasn't in the first act, so I found a spot in the wings to watch. The craziness of the plot drew me in, pulling me away from my real-life worries. The great thing about a play like A Midsummer Night's Dream is that it has such a dreamlike quality. Even the words sound foreign, like a song to which you don't know the lyrics but you understand the meaning.

The audience applauded when my first scene with Oberon ended. I raced backstage and used the minutes until my next scene to rehearse. When Act III started, I slipped onto the darkened stage and pretended to sleep through the love spell, sleep until donkey Reed showed up to awaken me. I kept my eyes shut—not too tight—and tried my best not to move.

Reed's deep voice sang a silly song. . . .

"The ousel-cock, so black of hue,
With orange-tawny bill . . ."

The stage vibrated with each oafish stomp. The audience was already laughing, hungry for comedic relief.

"The throstle with his note so true,
The wren with little quill . . ."

The sound of Bottom's voice ignited the love spell. My eyes fluttered open. *"What angel wakes me from my flowery bed?"*

Reed kept on singing. I squinted at him and my stomach dropped. Reed wasn't wearing his donkey head. Instead, he had on some makeshift ears and brown face paint. He smirked at me when he finished his song.

That's right. I'd been so focused on Façade business that I'd forgotten about Reed's lost donkey head. And now I was going to have to *kiss* him. That's how the scene ended. And no donkey head would be between us. We hadn't even rehearsed this! I'd never stage kissed! The last time I'd even made lip contact had been at the dunk tank. When Reed saved me. And I wasn't even conscious.

I made it through my lines. Celeste and the other fairies floated onto the stage, fawning over Bottom. The audience loved it—Reed could really ham it up. But then he said his last line, and it was my turn.

I stumbled over the first few words. Reed grabbed my hands and gave me a squeeze of encouragement, all the while looking at me with donkey love.

I ran my hand along the side of his face. With the

donkey head on, it was much funnier. Now it was almost . . . tender. He tipped his head to the side, like we'd practiced in rehearsals. So far, it was all like we'd practiced. Reed sings, I'm in love, the audience laughs, fairies dance, and . . . kiss.

We'd gone over it so many times, but this moment was different. Everyone was watching us, and Reed was watching me with his probing stare. His dark eyes. His waiting lips.

I stroked his cheek again and leaned in.

We kissed.

And the ground *shook*.

Or I did. Or he did. We did? I don't know. I don't know what happened. The kiss was only a couple of seconds, but I felt like I'd been flipped over and smacked in the face with a rainbow. Or something. All I know is, my emotions, my magic, went beyond buzzing. The energy shot out of my toes, my fingers . . . my lips. It was every magic moment I'd ever had, and then some.

It was . . . it was . . .

Just like kissing Karl. But *better*.

The stage went dark. We hurried off, and Reed grabbed my hand.

"Wow. Remind me to have a wardrobe malfunction more often."

I turned away. "I better go check my makeup."

"Wait." Reed rubbed the back of his neck. "I don't know how to say this, but . . . but did you feel something? Something, like . . ." His voice trailed off.

Magic, I wanted to say. But of course I didn't. I couldn't!

Not only was Reed my best friend's sort-of crush, I could never explain the feelings, the sensation pulsing through me right now. Unless, maybe, I was super tapped into Titania and my empathy was making *her* feel the love spell?

No. It was almost as if the strength or power of my magic had been multiplied. Doubled. Ugh, but that made no sense. This wasn't a magical marvel, this was a stage kiss in a high school play. It was nothing.

It had to be nothing.

"You're a terrific actor, Reed. I have to go."

I turned away and raced into the dressing room. Girls chattered and fiddled with each other's hair. Someone had written *All the world's a stage!* in lipstick across a vanity mirror. I wiped at it until I could see my face. Everything was going to be fine. Just a shock to the system. That's what happens when you don't practice without the donkey head.

I sat for a few minutes, listening to my cast mates, comforted by the rise and fall of meaningless conversation. My next part with Reed was only a scene away. It was hard enough talking to him after he'd saved my life; I didn't know how to face him now. Probably best to go talk first. Break the tension. Act like we hadn't kissed the world's greatest kiss.

I crept backstage, avoiding the groupings of techies and actors. Reed wasn't there, so I picked my way to the boys' dressing room. A sign on the door read NO PRANKS. STAY OUT.

I knocked, and when no one answered, pushed my way in. "Hello?"

Reed sat in a folding chair in the corner. He was bent

over, typing on something, and didn't look up when I came in. I took a step closer. The device in his hands looked like a cell phone. Kind of. There was a screen, some keys. Very high-tech. I would have thought it was some expensive electronic toy if I hadn't seen it before.

Except I knew it wasn't technological, but techno-*magical*.

Reed looked up and shoved his manual behind his back. "What? What is it?"

I took a step away. Reed had a manual. Which meant Reed was a sub. Wait, a SUB? It seemed totally impossible, but he had to be. Why else would he have a manual?

Specter. The secret agency branch. IT WAS BOYS. Princes, kings, maybe some dukes . . . male royalty subs. And the girls of Façade—Glimmer, that's what Meredith called our branch—had a natural rivalry with Specter boys.

Reed had left some unintentional clues. He traveled the world. And had lots of "acting" experience. And was always trying to size people up—the same as I would on a job. I bet he bolted at the skating rink when Kylee fell because his manual went off.

Holy Specter. HE HAD A MANUAL.

My head spun. That must have been why our contact felt so magical. It *was* magical. Double the magic. I slammed the door shut and leaned against it with my hands on my knees, so I wouldn't throw up. Reed opened the door slowly. I almost ran away, but stopped when he said my name.

"Desi. Sorry, I was just sending a text to my mom."

He thought it was a smooth lie, and it would have been in a different circumstance, with a non-magical person. He didn't know I had anything to do with Façade. Why would he? If I hadn't seen him using his manual myself, I would never have believed it.

"I'm glad you found me." He lowered his voice. "We need to talk about . . . Look, Desi, that kiss—"

"Can I see your phone?" Façade had a rule—you can't talk about Façade. But what if I didn't *say* anything? What if Reed found out by, uh, accident?

"No. It's my dad's and it's expensive. Sorry, he doesn't like anyone else using it."

"Yeah, I know. I have the same one."

Reed chuckled. "I doubt it."

"See?" I pulled out mine. "It gets great reception, huh?"

Of all the things I'd witnessed in the last few hours, the expression on Reed's face was the best. Poor guy looked like he'd swallowed his donkey head. My shock dissolved into giddiness. He stammered, "But, where did you . . . How did you . . . Are you a . . ."

"I have no idea what you're talking about," I said.

"Reed, Desi!" The stage manager hissed at us from the hallway. "Get out here. You two are on in a minute!"

We stood in the wings together, side by side. Reed's mouth was still agape.

"It makes sense if you think about it," I mused. "You get two people together who have you-know-what, and sparks are going to fly."

Reed's cue was about to start. He pointed at me and said, "Tonight. There's a party. And we're going to talk."

"Yes."

"Because this is crazy."

"Totally."

"Okay. Well." He tugged at a strand of my hair. "Good luck out there."

"You're not supposed to say that."

"Fine. How about . . ." He squinted at me. *"Here's looking at you, kid."*

The smile melted off my face. "What did you say?"

"It's a line. From a movie." He shrugged and burst onto the stage with a hee-haw.

It was a line. From *Casablanca*. The same line KARL had said to me when I was Elsa. The same line Karl didn't recognize when I said it to him as Floressa.

Which meant . . . nothing. Right? Lots of people know that line. Just because Reed said it, and Reed was a sub, it didn't mean he was . . . he was . . .

"You're on," the stage manager whispered.

I stumbled onto the stage. The lights were so bright. The theater packed. Reed gave me a quick, crooked smile, and I knew.

My crush on Karl was less complicated than I thought, because it wasn't *Karl* I'd been with that day in the garden.

Now, my crush on Reed . . . ?

That was scandal all its own.

Acknowledgments

riting a book is hard. Writing a second book? Harder. Or more difficult. Or just straight-up crazy-making. So I owe my sanity to the following people. Thank you all for helping me continue Desi's wild adventures. . . .

First, always first, my fabulous agent, Sarah Davies. Your understanding, calm, and caring are unmatched in this business.

Editors really should have their name somewhere on the cover as well. Emily Schultz, who championed Desi first and helped me establish the direction of this book and series. Catherine Onder, who is listed under DELIGHTFUL in the dictionary. Thank you for your keen eye, smart questions, and for keeping me calm and focused during crunch time. And Rachel Boden, for promoting the sparkle on the other side of the pond.

Hallie Patterson, Dina Sherman, Mollyanne M. Thomas, Nellie Kurtzman, and Ann Dye, THANK YOU for spreading the word near and far. Also, the rest of the folks at Disney-Hyperion—Sara Liebling, Marybeth Tregarthen, Marci Senders, and David Jaffe, Mark Amundsen, and Drew Richardson. You're a wonderful team, and I'm so glad to work with you all.

I wouldn't be able to write, period, if I didn't have help with my children (and if my children and family weren't so wonderful to begin with—go, team). Thanks for the babysitting from Carol Taylor, Jan Leavitt, Rachel and Spencer Orr, Claire and Liz Watson, Kaycie and Ravyn Brown, and especially Curry, a.k.a. Husband of the Century.

Beta-reader Caroline Thuet for helping me get into a tween girl's head. Ali Fredrick for your detailed insights on beauty pageants. The many schools and stores I've visited along the way—each place I've learned something new about the book and about me. And my writing friends! You know I would have checked out long ago without your doses of perspective.

Lastly, the readers. You are amazing. Your e-mails, notes, links, letters, pictures, tweets . . . I cherish every one. Thank you for being a part of the series. I get to do what I do because you are there.

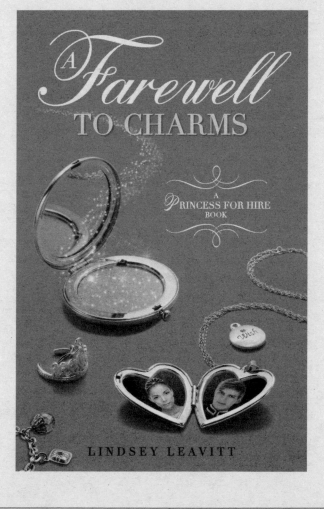

Chapter
I

A bead of cold sweat dangled on my fingertip before dripping onto the doorbell. What if I got electrocuted from my wet fingers? I would die literally inches away from my first high school party. And then everyone would be like, oh, poor thing was so nervous, what a tragedy. Death by sweat.

"Come on, Des," said my best friend, Kylee. "It's freezing out here."

Hypothermia *and* electrocution. Just to be safe, I knocked.

The door swung open. A muscular boy with acne and a sour expression leered at me. "Did you just try to ring the doorbell?"

"Uh . . . I knocked, actually," I said.

"No one knocks. What are you, a freshman?"

"We're in eighth grade," Kylee said.

"But *she* helps teach the high school band. She's a musical prodigy," I said.

Kylee punched me on the shoulder. "I hate when you call me a prodigy. I'm just advanced. I mean, musically advanced. It's not like I'm great at everything."

The guy still stood in the doorway, slack-jawed. Was he going to let us in? Was there some secret password we were supposed to say? Did we have to pay an admission fee?

"I'm in the cast," I said.

He blinked.

"For *A Midsummer Night's Dream*. I'm playing the fairy queen. Well, I guess *played*, since tonight was the final night."

"They cut the junior high theater program," Kylee added. "So Desi got to try out and made it—"

"And the assistant director said I could come. Because . . . because I'm in the cast," I finished. Lamely.

"I didn't ask for your résumé, theater freak. You people love to talk, don't you?" He let out a monstrous burp. "I'm crashing the party for the food."

He wandered away, leaving the door open. "Close the door!" someone yelled. "It's November—you want to freeze?"

We rushed inside.

"Great entrance." Kylee tucked a wisp of her black hair behind her ear. "Now we're the clueless, knocking eighth graders."

"I'll make us T-shirts that say that."

We *were* pretty clueless. Everyone in the cast probably thought it was a miracle that I actually got a part in this play. When, really, it wasn't much of a miracle. My work experience as a magical princess substitute meant acting came easily for me.

Yeah, I said magical princess substitute.

Not that anyone knew about my job with the Façade Agency, not even Kylee. The only people aware of my career were the royals I worked for and other Façade employees. The big shocker that I'd just discovered last week was that one of my cast mates, Reed Pearson, was also a substitute for royalty.

Reed was the reason I was here. We needed to finally talk about our magical coincidence. This party provided such a perfect opportunity to be alone that I'd risked the humiliation of having my parents drive me here. I'd insisted that they drop Kylee and me off a block away. My mom waved excitedly out the window while my dad stopped the car one last time to go over who to call in case of an emergency. This was after I'd talked him out of coming inside with us to speak to the parents of the party-thrower. Whoever that was.

I tugged down on my SHAKESPEARE ROCKETH T-shirt, surveying the house's open floor plan. It wasn't like the high school parties I'd seen in movies—no one was swinging from chandeliers, and the furniture was still in place. No DJ or dancing either. Everyone was spread out around the house—talking on the couch, eating in the kitchen. The mood resembled parties we had in junior high, except the conversations were more . . . mature. I caught one snippet between two seniors about college applications. *College.*

"So, what are we supposed to do now?" Kylee asked.

"I don't know," I said. "Mingle?"

"There's a horror movie that starts out like this, you know. *Party of the Dead.* These nerdy girls show up at this party that they think is full of popular people, but actually demons possessed all the cool kids' bodies—"

"Coach Kylee!" Steve, a junior who'd played the part of King Oberon, slapped Kylee on the back. Steve was nice enough, but he acted like he was on a stage twenty-four/ seven. "Did you come to give me a private oboe lesson?"

Kylee's face reddened. "I'm here with Desi. I know it's a cast party, but she didn't want to come alone, so I—"

"I'm glad you came," he said. "Have we ever even talked? Ninety percent of the time we're around each other you're blowing on an instrument. Not the best conversation starter."

Kylee giggled. I thought he might be flirting with her, but I couldn't tell. In junior high, boys still insulted the girls they liked. Or didn't like. It was all very confusing.

"Come on, I'll introduce you to my magical fairy court. You already know my wife, Titania." He pointed at me and lowered his voice. "We're in a little bit of a tiff. She has a crush on a donkey."

I rolled my eyes. Always acting.

"He was looking for you, actually," Steve said.

"Who, Reed?" I asked.

"Yeah. He probably wants another smooch." He swung his arm around Kylee. "Go find him. I'm stealing Kylee."

Great. Steve had to bring up the kissing. It was a stage kiss during one single, solitary performance, and the only reason it had happened was because Reed had misplaced his costume donkey head. And, okay, yes, the kiss was magical, but it wasn't *real*. Reed also gave me mouth-to-mouth last summer when I nearly drowned in a dunk tank, and no one was making snarky comments about *that*.

Kylee's smile faltered. "Oh, so you go talk to Reed, then. Alone, I guess."

"He's probably going to critique my performance tonight." I shrugged. It was a heavy shrug. "He's always doing that."

"Well, tell him I said hi," Kylee said. "And maybe . . . Well, just hi."

"So, do you help the band director with our grades at all?" Steve asked as he guided Kylee outside to a hodgepodge of lawn chairs circling a fire pit.

This Reed thing was going to get sticky. Kylee had liked him since he'd first moved to Idaho last June. We'd spent hours strategizing ways to "run into him," and every time we did, Kylee froze. She'd probably said three sentences to him. Total. She claimed she was going to get over her crush, but it's not that easy. If feelings could be controlled, then I wouldn't like the same guy my best friend liked.

Not that I admitted it to Kylee. And I'd only recently figured out that *Reed* was the boy I liked when I discovered that he worked for Façade and might just be my long-lost Prince Charming. I don't mean that in a cutesy way, either. I'd fallen for Prince Karl while on a job in the Alps, and I'm pretty sure Reed was substituting for him at the time. I still needed to talk to Reed about it, but how could I bring that up? *Hey, Reed, have you ever fallen for a princess while subbing who wasn't really the royal you thought? You have? Yay! That was me! Let's get married! Or at least get a milk shake.*

See? Sticky.

I finally spotted Reed hovering over a bowl of Skittles. He was wearing a fitted gray T-shirt, his olive skin practically glowing in the brightly lit kitchen. It had been two weeks since our stage kiss, followed by two weeks of performances (and two weeks of avoidance because the weirdness was too much). This moment was the reason I was here, but I couldn't quite convince my feet to move.

Reed looked up, and our eyes locked. And then it didn't matter if I could move or not, because he was already crossing the room. As he walked past our cast mates, they gave him high fives or brayed in honor of his role of Bottom, the donkey. He smiled and laughed, but the whole time he was staring at me.

"Hey," he said, his voice soft. His gaze, so focused on me before, now bounced around the room.

I don't know how many times we'd said *hey* or *hello* or *hi* during rehearsals. I couldn't count them because they hadn't mattered. But now everything seemed to matter—his hair, his mouth, and the way his New Zealand accent managed to make the word "hey" sound beautiful. He was the same, but totally new.

I smiled. "Hey."

He held up his arms like he was displaying something to the left of him. "What do you think?"

I blinked at the blank space. "What do I think about what?"

"This lovely elephant in the room." Reed pretended to pet the air. "What should we name him? Something like e-way are-way oth-bay oyal-ray ubs-say?"

Pig Latin. We are both royal subs. Yeah, it was the elephant between us—the truth that we hadn't yet been able to discuss—but the funny thing was that we were the only ones at this party aware of our secret.

"I thought we weren't supposed to talk about . . . where we work." I glanced around the party, worried that my agent, Meredith, was going to pop out of her traveling bubble at any moment. "Faça . . . I mean, our boss watches us, you know."

Reed patted his fake pet. "You know what's great about invisible elephants? They're easy to make disappear. Come on."

He grabbed my hand, and we dodged through the guests. My first high school party and I was already holding a guy's hand! Who, okay, was only leading me away so we could discuss magic, but it still gave me a thrill. Part of me thought to let go, in case Kylee saw, but my fingers wouldn't listen to that rational part of my brain. Fingers are tricky like that.

Reed pounded on the door of a bathroom and led me inside.

"Don't tell me we're giving the elephant a bath now," I said.

Reed hit some buttons on his manual, a small touch-screen computer that had all the information we needed about the agency and our clients. He was using this device when I'd first put together his connection to Façade.

"I need yours," Reed said.

When he was done punching keys on my manual, he blew air through his nose. "No interruptions—I muted Central Command's surveillance on us. Anytime we're together with our manuals now, it'll block out our conversation. Just try not to look suspicious so they zoom in to lip-read when they figure out there isn't any noise."

"You can do that?"

"Little technical loophole I picked up along the way. There are all sorts of hidden applications on here. I just downloaded a key system that allows me access to anywhere in our Specter offices—I'm sure you could find one for Façade, too. And I've heard about some sort of scanner you can use to check if a royal is real or a sub. Haven't figured that one out yet."

"Yeah, but . . . does Façade care? Those kind of applications give the subs too much power."

"The agency put the apps on the phone. Of course we can use them. Besides"—he gave me a funny look—"we're employees, not fugitives. We still have the right of privacy."

I wasn't so sure about that. Façade did some questionable things to hopeful employees who didn't meet their standards. During my last agency visit, I'd found the sub-sanitation room, the place where potential subs' magic was unknowingly stripped and stored for Façade purposes. I had no clue how many people had endured this treatment, or if there were dangerous side effects. I didn't know what to do with the information—if I should keep quiet or try to stop Façade. I hoped Reed would help me find the courage to decide what to do. I just had to open up to him first.

"They can still see us," I whispered.

"If they're watching. The sub security device Façade uses is a roving radar. And they have much more important things to do than watch two subs talking about elephants at a cast party."

"But, say they *are* watching, shouldn't we be somewhere less suspicious? Like out there, eating Skittles, instead of in a bathroom? They're less likely to watch if we're acting normal."

"True. Wow, you're really paranoid."

Reed would be paranoid too if he knew what I knew about Façade. "Professional. Not paranoid."

"I thought it'd be nice if we could . . . be alone," Reed said. "I mean, to talk." We both didn't say anything for a bit. The silence was awkward but exhilarating. Reed wanted to be alone with me! Even if it was in a small bathroom with peeling floral wallpaper. He eased onto the edge of the bathtub and motioned to the toilet seat. "Now I finally have you here, and we're safe. So sit. And tell me everything."